A COOL DAY FOR KILLING

'Grant a writer the possession of one gift in real abundance,' said H. R. F. Keating reviewing Haggard's last novel in *The Times*, 'and that solitary talent will of itself lift us time and again into space-cleaving orbit. Such a writer is William Haggard. His gift is simply that he cannot put pen to paper without showing in every word and letter an unchippable top-level establishment viewpoint. Whatever particular story he embarks on he takes you in it with superb naturalness into the highest of high places. It is an entrancing gift. The highest places are of their nature small places. There is not room in them for all of us, except by proxy. Mr Haggard is our proxy in the seats of power.'

In Haggard's new top-level thriller Charles Russell, Head of the Security Executive, moves into the murkier under-currents of diplomacy with a discretion dictated by a highly delicate situation.

To the embarrassment of the British Government and, more particularly, to Russell's Minister, the Malay State of Shahbaddin, for a century and more under British protection, has grown ripe for Chinese plucking. In London the Kensington office of His Excellency the High Commissioner of Shahbaddin is the centre of intrigue. It is also, since it ranks as an Embassy, undeniably foreign soil. Which proves a somewhat disconcerting circumstance when both the daughter and the nephew of the murdered British ruler of Shahbaddin are enticed, with oriental cunning, beyond its impregnable doors. For Charles Russell the challenge is not one to be lightly dismissed.

A COOL DAY

WILLIAM HAGGARD

FOR KILLING

CASSELL · LONDON

CASSELL & COMPANY LTD
35 Red Lion Square, London WC1
Melbourne, Sydney, Toronto
Johannesburg, Auckland

© William Haggard 1968
First published 1968

S.B.N. 304 93198 5

Printed in Great Britain by
The Camelot Press Ltd, London and Southampton
F. 668

PROLOGUE

Outside the palace it was ominously quiet. It wasn't in fact a palace either architecturally or in its ambience but a comfortable hot-weather bungalow in a palm grove by the sea. The real palace was in the capital, a colonial rococo horror in the taste of the 1880s. His Highness, the fifth of his line, hardly noticed the greenhouse heat of the sweating little capital but he had the love of his race for the sea and the beach and would come to this modest bungalow as the richer of his subjects would escape at weekends to their pretentious country club. The veranda was wide, the living-room really, and sometimes a faint breeze cooled it.

His Highness sat in it now in a long cane chair. He was waiting to die and he wasn't too much afraid of death.

He wasn't afraid of dying—his religion had taught him that. He was the fifth of his line and the fourth in Islam. His great-great-grandfather had arrived in this sweltering land in the clothes he stood up in and nothing more, the penniless wandering Scot of his age and class, and this out-of-a-ship ship's engineer had carved himself a kingdom. He hadn't set out to do so, only to make a fortune, but empire had been in the air of the time, pervasive as pollen and as troublesome to its victims, and a Queen had accepted his son as liegeman. 'Accepted' was how they'd phrased it though in fact he'd been compelled. Sir Robert Harry Raden, first baronet, courtesy Highness.

The second Raden had been unimpressed for he'd stayed a Scot. He'd loved his preposterous fief, he'd liked the people, but since a widow he'd never seen had made him a prince he'd damned well be one. His father had been born on the land of an absentee duke and he wouldn't have that, by God he wouldn't. No, he'd identify, do the job properly. His people were Moslem, their ruler should be the same. He hadn't considered apostasy since he'd never set foot in Scotland. The kirk, solemn elders, the grim doctrines of Geneva—all these meant nothing. He'd been received into Islam and his children and children's children had followed easily.

And now his great-grandson was waiting for death, His Highness Lieutenant Colonel Sir Montagu Raden, Baronet, D.S.O, Knight This, Knight That. . . .

He'd forgotten the tally of letters and badges: they came up with the rations anyway. The D.S.O. he'd earned, the rest were chaff.

He had more important things to think of than something they threw you when a young woman was crowned or an honour to mark some boring princeling's visit to Shahbaddin. He was considering death. Life too.

He hadn't had a bad one, he was ready to go uncomplainingly. He hadn't expected to inherit, but an elder brother had died unexpectedly. Five tropical generations had left the Radens white in blood; they went home for their wives if not too strictly for their mistresses, steady girls of good blood and bone, women to breed from. And Sir Montagu's father had had a horror of idleness, of younger sons in pampered ease, of palace revolutions. So Montagu Raden had been a regular British officer. He'd enjoyed it in peacetime, though he'd hated the war. He wasn't, he knew, alone in that, but as a major he'd won a D.S.O., and that had been far from easy.

. . . All right, so he'd done his stuff. What else?

It had been a good life while it lasted. Ceremonial duties in London were a bore, but there'd been the easy male companionship and astonishing tolerance. A mountain of rubbish was talked about the army, or at least about Raden's part of it. He'd been a Moslem—who cared? He didn't drink—who asked him to? When there were sausages his own were always beef. They'd managed the whole thing effortlessly. He'd been Montagu Raden, a pretty good soldier.

And now he was the Ruler and quite soon he was going to die.

Well, he was decently organized. The army had taught him that, a dislike of avoidable messiness. He was heirless and now was glad of it. His daughter would be all right. She'd been living in Shahbaddin but he had sent her back to England when her mother had died three years ago, unwilling to keep a daughter chained as old age inexorably stalked him. There was a trust which would look after her and in any case she'd marry. Sir Montagu smiled. Sheila would marry—oh yes, indeed. And lucky the man who won her. Sheila was a honey-pot and she needn't marry for money.

He clapped his hands and a servant came in quietly. Raden could tell nothing from his manner. The Malay had the deceptive softness of his race, a pride in service wholly innocent of obsequiousness. He wouldn't be Raden's executioner, it wouldn't be seemly for a man to kill his master, but he would know what was in the wind, its day and hour. It would be useless to ask, improper too. The smiling well-trained face was a mask.

Sir Montagu sipped his lime juice. In a sense it was all unnecessary. He was perfectly conscious that he was an anachronism, but he wasn't a reactionary and he'd been ready to go decently. But not in that way, that dishonest and shameful way. There'd been that shoddy little man they'd sent out from England, a junior Minister from an office of little weight. He'd been brash and ingratiating, not quite at ease and at the same time a bully. Sir Montagu had detested him. And beneath the evasions, what had been the proposition? Raden still wasn't sure, for the double-talk had confused him. Something about vesting his hereditary powers in a representative body. What did that mean in simple words? Well. . . . He'd keep his title of course, but in practice he'd be powerless. Could he stay in the country? Well again. . . . It would be better if he left but if he insisted it might be negotiable.

And what did *that* mean? Not much, it seemed. He must leave and then they'd talk.

3

Like hell he would; he wasn't another white rajah. He had a house in Hampshire where he went for the winter shooting, but England without a job would be simple hell. He wouldn't be happy in Hampshire, not a Moslem, not a foreigner. They'd come to his home but he wouldn't fit. It wouldn't be like his regiment, not a bit.

Besides, he loved his people. This was his home, his roots, his active life.

He'd sent the junior Minister packing and the pressure had come on smoothly. The plan had been to shelve him, join his awkward little patrimony into a larger federation. He thought little of federations, or not the sort the British contrived. They left more problems than they appeared to solve and besides, it was running away. After five generations one simply didn't. And that terrible little Minister, that vulgar fixer. . . .

Outside in the garden he saw a man move. For a moment Raden stiffened, then he recognized the mover. It was one of the gardeners and they wouldn't use him. That wouldn't be local form at all. They wouldn't use a man's servant nor the servant consent if they tried. If his people had asked him themselves he'd have gone in peace, his imam for instance, or the elders of his council whom he respected. But they never would. Perhaps London would have suggested it but it would have been contemptuously rejected if it had. Sir Montagu knew his people, and not as some intellectual exercise; he was quite without race-feeling, despised it wholly. He respected his subjects, a respect they returned. Their manners were far too good to consider humiliating him. To kill him, though. . . .

But that would be rather different. One might kill but one mustn't offend.

Sir Montagu Raden wondered how it would come. Would London know? It would know and it wouldn't—that was the Whitehall way. His death would suit them beautifully but they'd turn away their eyes from it. If he asked for protection they'd prevaricate and delay. In any case he never would. British soldiers, perhaps the sons of men he'd known, stamping

4

about in his garden with guns, shadowing him on his evening walk. . . .

He'd lose so much face he'd rather die. Five generations in Shahbaddin made face important.

He sipped again at his lime juice, resigned. One thing was certain, they'd do it decently. The knife was the local weapon but death by the knife could be painful. He was certain they wouldn't wish him pain, so they'd hire some Chinese gunman from the mainland and let him shoot. Then they'd pay the man the sum agreed, throwing it at his feet, not touching his person. If he gave them so much as a look they'd kill him too. The new wind had blown and the people wanted change, political change and he stood in the way. Fair enough, so he'd have to go. But they wouldn't behave discourteously.

Raden looked at his watch, smiling ironically. In half an hour he'd be saying his evening prayers, facing the west on his fine Ghiordes prayer rug, turning his back to the garden, bowing. To a Chinese behind a flowering shrub the target would be a tempting one.

Sir Montagu Raden laughed aloud. A Chinese who shot a praying man would be unlikely to live the night out.

He finished his drink but delayed to rise. He was waiting for the call to prayer. It was just, he was thinking—he couldn't escape. It was written upon his forehead and that was that. He had no heir. There was Oliver, his dead brother's son, but Oliver was a bastard. A foolish impertinent word but the English thought it important. Marriage was a contract, not a sacrament as the Christians taught, but Oliver wasn't in legal line so Oliver didn't count. The poor English had been brainwashed by the Nazarene's misinterpreters. Also they might be making a great mistake. Oliver was a Raden and though his mother hadn't been English her blood was good. Raden and upper-crust Malay—the mixture could be interesting when it wasn't simply degenerate, and Oliver Kendry was emphatically not degenerate. Sir Montagu Raden smiled again. His father's butler had been called Kendry, and Oliver's mother would no more have slept with him than she would with a Chinese. But one had to preserve the form of things, especially with Whitehall round one's neck. Raden wondered where Oliver was, he'd been lying low.

He rose at the evening call to prayer but halted at a tiny noise. Two men were in the veranda now, Chinese as he'd expected. He could see they were armed and they knew their weapons. Good. He hadn't been taught that suffering ennobled. He nodded to them politely and they shot him down in silence.

CHAPTER ONE

Colonel Charles Russell of the Security Executive had been summoned by his Minister, and Harry Tuke was watching him shrewdly. Tuke treated Russell with the casual respect of an equal (this Russell noticed) but also with a private and quite genuine affection which he concealed. He saw in his leather armchair a man of mature but still vigorous middle age, much more than a senior civil servant, much less than just another secret policeman. Harry Tuke was a realist and it didn't disturb him that Russell's background was precisely what in public he derided, the land-owning Anglo-Irish family, the service in a part of Her Majesty's forces which men to the Left of him would happily see disbanded. Even if these had troubled him Harry Tuke was far too sensible to allow them to weigh in practice: on the contrary they were advantages, for the post of head of the Executive was a difficult one to fill. Its work was an essential to any state which wished to remain one, but the rule of law was a sacred cow, at any rate in public, and the man who bent it or pulled its nose could be broken and disowned next day. Not could be but must be: that is, if he failed or, much worse, were uncovered. There were plenty of men who'd accept that risk but they weren't the sort of men you could safely trust. Charles Russell was. This handsome, tolerant, civilized man might be suspect of another age, but he was also discreet and disciplined and he was wholly without ambition. He didn't need to be ambitious since he had most things he'd ever valued. Absurd old-fashioned values such as unflinching private loyalty? Perhaps, but Tuke didn't think so. Charles Russell was a powerful man—just how much power he held few knew—but he had a fastidious distaste for its arbitrary exercise. That the Security Executive existed at all

7

was a commentary on dangerous times, its name a byword and a hissing to what Tuke privately thought of as softy fools. But since it had to exist you had to find a head for it, and better by far this scrupulous, pleasantly dated man than some painfully with-it contemporary committed in private to God knew what.

Charles Russell for his part thought that Tuke was a man you could do business with. He had a party of course, but he was a Minister of the Crown, and he was very much more interested in the realities of the latter than in the polemics of party politics, the disturbance and dust of annual conventions. All parties had a centre line, and it was a maxim in Mr Harry Tuke's that its centre point lay where Harry Tuke stood. He was clever, too, at managing men. There were men to the Left who alarmed him and, worse, were boring, but he'd always avoided their malice. As Cabinet colleagues to his Right had not. He was always polite with fools, the Pauline gift, ready to listen, pat backs and be matey. Later he'd wash his hands and take a drink. Good old Harry, you could trust him.

Charles Russell trusted him also. For somewhat subtler reasons and on rather severer tests he liked Harry Tuke and played ball with him happily. Harry Tuke was a professional, Harry Tuke was a cool old hand. He was saying now politely:

'It was good of you to come so promptly.'

'At your service. For what it's worth.' Russell wasn't apologetic, merely factual. Ministers often asked the impossible.

'It's all rather vague, annoyingly untidy.'

'It mostly is.'

'I know—so do you. That's the reason we get on admirably.' The Minister drank a cup of very dark tea. Charles Russell had declined it. 'It's about Shahbaddin.'

'A bit out of my manor. I've read what's been in the papers but nothing else. But it's possible something's cooking. You want me to send a man there?'

'No.'

8

'Good. Since I haven't one suitable.'

The Minister poured another cup of the shattering brew he drank like water. 'You were right that there's something blowing up. Mind if I start at the beginning?'

'It's usually best,' Charles Russell said dryly.

'Then Shahbaddin was an anachronism. In the early nineteenth century a Scottish adventurer called Raden arrived there with his shirt-tails out of his trousers. He had a talent for trading and he made himself a fortune, but he also had an itch to put things straight.' The Minister laughed. 'Nowadays it's called a talent for administration, and if you don't control it carefully it lands you in the Cabinet. So this Raden arrives on a sleepy little coast with nothing there. There was some sort of rascally sultan, but he'd gone a bit too far even for local tolerance. He died rather suddenly in circumstances which have never been investigated. The Radens took over—local potentates, Mark Two.'

'Mark Two till they were recognized.'

'Quite so. It was the Victorians did it, naturally. They had a passion for real estate. So the Radens became baronets, and they had nineteen guns in their own absurd territory.' The Minister looked up. 'Now you can't get away with that in the 1960s.'

'I don't see why not.'

'You're pulling my leg, Charles. Even Tory Prime Ministers make asses of themselves with speeches about the wind of change. We're supposed to breathe it naturally.'

'And do you?'

'It's an un-question. What I breathe is the air which comes to me. That's practical politics, the art of the possible.'

Russell said quietly: 'The last Raden was assassinated. That must have been convenient.'

'Only because he wouldn't go. There's a mystery there and perhaps you could explain it. Why he wouldn't go, I mean.'

'I shot with him twice in Hampshire but I didn't know him well.'

'You were men of the same background. The same class, if you'll forgive me.'

'I won't—the word means nothing.' Charles Russell pulled his grey moustache, then asked the Minister blandly: 'And what were you offering as bait to get him out?'

'Frankly, almost nothing. We were going to strip him of power. He'd have kept his title and an income but nothing more.'

'Just like one of those miserable Indian rajahs.' The head of the Executive reflected calmly. 'And would you have let him stay in Shahbaddin?'

'It wasn't a term of the contract that he should leave. But we should have had to ease him out.'

'Which he'd realize, of course?'

'He was nobody's fool.'

'Then I don't think you handled it cleverly, not at all. If you'd gone there yourself——'

'How could I go? I may be a Minister, but I'm nothing to do with what's left of the Empire.'

'You could have stopped them sending Willis.'

'*Touché*. Willis is young and a pompous theorist.' The Minister looked at Russell hard. 'Do *you* fancy Willis?'

'No.'

'Would Willis have persuaded you?'

Charles Russell shook his head.

'Then you've answered my question. Thank you.'

There was an understanding silence which Russell broke. 'So now there's a sort of parliament, a prime minister, all the trimmings.'

'And they're in the Federation.'

'Bad. If you don't mind my reminding you, we haven't been very successful with federations.'

'But this one has an outside chance.'

'And why?'

'Because it's got an enemy, an immediate, material enemy. The others had enemies too but they weren't a danger. They were bogeys, not the needed glue, words like neo-colonialism, plus the understandable incompetence of slaves turned suddenly master. But Shahbaddin is actively threatened.'

'By whom?'

'Charles, you're not an innocent. Forty per cent of the population of Shahbaddin is Chinese. The Chinese don't mix racially and they're very uneasy bedfellows for what's supposed to be a bi-racial state.'

'You're worried they'll try and take over? With or without help from the mother country?'

'We're *all* very worried. And another thing's just come up. It's a girl called Sheila Raden, the last Raden Ruler's daughter.'

'You can't seriously think that she's planning some *coup*.' Charles Russell was incredulous. 'I've met her and she's a beauty, but she's only twenty-two. Also, if I may remind you, Shahbaddin's a Moslem country.'

'No, you're jumping to conclusions. But do you ever read the Law Reports?'

'Never unless I have to.'

'Then Montagu Raden had estate in this country. There's been trouble about it—plenty.'

'I never monkey with the civil law. The criminal sometimes, it's part of the job. But the Chancery courts are not my patch.'

'You're going too fast so I'll buy you lunch.'

They ate, as Russell feared they would, in Harry Tuke's club. He had chosen it carefully since he couldn't risk the impression that he was either rich or frivolous. He despised inverted snobbery but there were people in his party who did not, and he was a successful politician and therefore careful of his image. He had chosen the Refectory though he knew the food was terrible.

Russell looked round the shabby-grand dining-room. They had started with potted shrimps and they weren't quite fresh. The Minister asked: 'You've been here before?'

'Oh yes, indeed.' Russell might have added, but did not, that if Tuke hadn't been his Minister he'd have found some excuse to eat elsewhere. At the table beside them were two senior civil servants. They were eating in total silence, drinking

Graves from a carafe. There was cold chicken salad and mayonnaise from a bottle.

Charles Russell suppressed a shudder.

'What do you think of it?'

'It *has* something. Undeniably.' Russell was a tactful man or he wouldn't have lasted a week in his job.

'And what would you say was the something?'

'An air of the past, of faded glories. And I prefer my glories faded.'

'The great days of Liberalism? Gladstone in the smoking-room?'

'I suppose that's it.'

'And it's exactly what worries me.'

Russell said involuntarily: 'Then why did you join?'

'I didn't mean the club, I meant Shahbaddin.'

'I'm afraid I'm not with you.'

Mr Harry Tuke leant forward. He had finished his shrimps but Russell had not. For a moment he was the Minister but Russell didn't resent it. 'Stop fencing and listen. We're the same sort of man, not Gladstonian Liberals; we like to see the wheels go round and alas we can't send gunboats.' The Minister finished a gin and tonic. 'And the wheels could get jammed in Shahbaddin.'

'But I thought you were hopeful.'

'I am. Provided we can keep it afloat. Three years and it might be viable.'

A waitress brought colf beef, overdone, and Russell pecked. 'I'm listening.'

'When the Radens went to Shahbaddin it was a tropical slum in the best Greene manner. The natives were Malays and I like Malays. Admittedly they're not pushful, they're lousy soldiers and worse administrators, but as you said of this club, they have something. They can be tricky but they're gentle, and they laugh a lot and love the sun. They're not morally smug like Indians and their manners are superb. They'll knife you in the back no doubt, but they'll give you a greeting doing it. . . . What are you drinking to keep alive?'

12

'Beer please.'

'So what the first Raden found was a Malay colony from the mainland, and the family built it up into a flourishing little patrimony. So of course the Chinese moved in *en masse*, just as they had on the mainland itself. And you know the Chinese. I like the Malays but I can't say I respect them; I respect the Chinese but I can't say I like them. They're hardworking and materialist and clannish and very tough. Any Chinese can make rings round a dozen Malays. And does.'

'The same situation as on the mainland, in fact?'

'Not quite. Shahbaddin's smaller and it's very much nearer China.'

'Then may I inquire the state of play?'

'You may. The present government's a balance between Malay and Chinese interests, but Malays being what they are its future is pretty precarious. If the Chinese upset the balance they might well do something embarrassing, such as leaving the Federation, asking for, well, protection from a Power which wouldn't suit our book. Or anyone's for that matter. Not even Russia—no, especially not Russia.'

'It's gone as far as that?'

'We've got to tread very carefully for the next few years. That's where this girl comes in.'

Russell said thoughtfully: 'There was some sort of bastard nephew, I hear, but he wasn't interested in politics. Anyway, he isn't recognized.' He drank some beer. 'But you told me you weren't suggesting that this girl had a finger in the Shahbaddin pie.'

'I did and I meant it. I'm simply suggesting that she's the heir to her father's property in this country.' Tuke leant forward again, wagging a forefinger. '*Which the state of Shahbaddin is claiming some of as its own.*'

'Let them fight it in the courts then.'

'Well spoken as an Englishman.' The Minister grinned. 'Have you ever tried to explain the rule of law to a Malay?'

'I can't say I have.'

'Then don't. We've already been asked for help and we're

13

on a spot. The High Commissioner won't accept that we're powerless to intervene. His government expects our help and to them we're simply withholding it. So they'll start thinking about their own positions, wondering what we'd be good for in a really serious pinch. Then they'll start guessing which way the cat will jump, wondering which race would come out top. The present lot is tired and shaky but at least it's a formal balance. If it decided we were no good to them I'd guess it would sell out quickly. And then——'

'I'm glad I'm not a Minister.'

'I'm equally glad I'm not Charles Russell.'

'But you're asking me to do something. Nobble a judge perhaps and cheat the girl? For reasons of high policy no doubt, but cheat the girl?'

Charles Russell had sounded irritated but the Minister didn't rise to it. 'Not that,' he said smoothly, 'or not just yet. But I thought you ought to know.'

'Know what?'

'Come off it, Charles, you're not a child. We want Shahbaddin to survive and as part of the Federation. We can't back one race openly, that's not in the modern rules, but if they think that we're letting them down it could start the slide.'

'I see. But I've still a question.'

'Yes?'

'What do I do?'

'You watch,' Tuke said. 'You watch and pray.'

'I'll watch all right. You pray.'

Sheila Raden was on her way to her solicitors. They were Lewis and Lee and she knew she was lucky, but she didn't know quite how lucky she was in fact. They'd been her father's advisers and she'd slipped on to their books quite naturally, thinking that she was fortunate to have anyone quite so eminent still interested in a client no longer famous. In this she was mistaken but she was also very young. Lewis and Lee were eminent but not the sort of firm to drop the daughter of a dead client, and apart from their legal standing they were also something special. Their reputation was one of a matchless probity; it even pleased them to be thought a little stuffy. They knew how to flatter counsel, how to stroke an old judge's whiskers, but behind the smooth and old-fashioned façade was a bottomless contempt for the law's masquerade. Not one of them would have admitted it, no one from senior partner to articled clerk, but the unspoken assumption in Lewis and Lee was that the law was an ass, its practitioners pompous donkeys. Behind their flawless reputation they were quietly and grimly ruthless. On their clients' behalf—that went without saying—and they were choosy about their clients. But once you were in you were in for life, with all the advantages of a deceptively fusty orthodoxy to mask the remorseless drive of a firm of immigrant twisters. Not that Lewis and Lee were a Rosenkrantz, Klein and Sligo. No court would trust a firm called that but everyone thought the earth of Lewis and Lee.

Its waiting-list was longer than White's club.

Sheila was shown into a waiting-room with fresh flowers and the latest papers. A secretary brought her a tea-tray—not a cuppa but a tea-tray. Presently she was called to David Marks. She'd seen a senior partner first, her father's friend, but he'd suggested very tactfully that she might be happier with a younger man. She'd accepted the hint at once, by no means embarrassed. Senior partners could be busy men and a junior might serve her better. She was a beauty and knew it, prepared to trade.

David Marks rose to greet her. He was a taut young Jew behind severe-looking spectacles, dressed, not as she'd expected in black coat and spongebag trousers, but in elegant effortless tweeds which said seventy guineas and lucky to pay it. 'Please be seated,' he said formally.

Sheila Raden sat down.

David Marks made small talk, thinking. He had a file on the Radens and had been reading it carefully, but the instincts of his race told him more about Sheila Raden than any file. Besides, he was wholly male. She sat in her chair demurely, but conscious of power, of womanhood. Few English girls did that very well but then she wasn't standard English. He took off his glasses, which in fact were a prop, and looked at her. The girl had a sort of glow, like the women of his own race, he thought, a sort of innocent invitation. Sensational! A pity that he was a Jew and she a Moslem.

'Where would you like me to start?' he asked.

'Wherever you think best. I don't understand much.'

She wouldn't, he realized, have to. Ever. Not with that body.

'Then let's start with the trust, the one your father set up for you. My most senior partner is one of the trustees, and the other is Clement Addis. That's Mastertons, you know—the jewellers. Where your father kept his jewellery in a safe.'

'If there was any worthwhile jewellery.'

. . . So she wasn't only a body, she'd got a mind. He'd have taken her gladly for body alone. Some lucky Gentile bastard, some Moslem oaf. . . .

'We're going a bit too quick. Let's assume that safe's full of jewellery. To which you hold a grant of probate.'

'I understand that bit, Sir John explained yesterday.'

'So we took out a grant for you. That wasn't difficult. There was a perfectly normal will, and you were the residuary to your father's estate in this country.'

'Residuary?'

'I'm sorry—the jargon creeps up on you. In ordinary languge you get everything he had here after one or two small gifts. There's a nephew, I believe, but he's been provided for already.'

'Oliver Kendry, really Oliver Raden. I'm glad he's been provided for.'

'You knew him well?'

'Pretty well when I was a child. Barring the English colony Shahbaddin was a tolerant place, and my grandfather's house was a sensible sort of home.' She said it without a smile, as a matter of fact.

'I understand you perfectly.' A Jew, he did. 'May I ask when you last saw him?'

'When I was last in Shahbaddin. That would be three years

ago, but we didn't meet as much as we did once. He was older, you see—thirty-six or thirty-seven.'

She made it sound like ninety-nine and David Marks flinched visibly. He was coming up for thirty-four.

'We're getting a bit off the point, which is the grant which we hold to your father's estate. Your trust isn't part of it, but there's a house and some jewellery. That's perfectly simple, or rather it was. It was until the authorities in Shahbaddin claimed that that safe at Mastertons is stuffed with the crown jewels.'

'That's nonsense—there weren't any. We weren't that sort of family.'

'I believe you entirely, but there's a man called the High Commissioner who doesn't. He went to the court and got something called an injunction.'

'I'm afraid I don't follow that bit.'

'It's regrettably simple. If that safe has anything in it there'll be a court case about who owns it, the State of Shahbaddin and Sheila Raden as executrix. Meanwhile there's this injunction, which means that nobody can dispose of whatever the wretched safe contains.'

'Not even me?'

'Especially not you.' He smiled with a hint of irony now. 'Though as a matter of fact you're hardly on the breadline yet. The grant covers all the property, the injunction only the safe, so you're free to sell the house whenever you wish. The High Commissioner isn't interested in the house. He's interested in the safe though, and since Mastertons held the safe he went for them.'

'What happened?'

David Marks said sardonically: 'The normal nonsense. Old Addis was summoned to chambers, where he gave the usual undertakings that nothing would leave the safe until the suit had been decided. Most impressive old man—the judge loved him dearly. One gentleman to another, you know, the word of a firm like Mastertons. It was all very matey, reassuring if that's your taste in law, emetic if it isn't. It took seven minutes flat and his lordship was lavish with compliments.'

'Of course he was, they were saving him trouble.'

'What did you say?' He had sat up sharply.

She seemed surprised. 'I said they were saving the judge-man trouble.'

'If you ever want legal work you can come right here.'

'I might one day if we lose this case.'

'I'm not worried about these absurd crown jewels. Like you I don't believe in them. The danger is that that safe may contain a considerable pile of quite ordinary family jewellery. Suppose it does, can you prove it was your father's?'

'I can prove the family used it.'

'That may not be enough.'

'Then we're going to lose?'

'No, I didn't say that. Your family dealt with Mastertons for generations and there's plenty of evidence where most things will have come from. Why, we've traced a tiara which your grandfather bought in the 1910s. He paid with his own cheque at that, on his personal account at a bank in St James's. Of course they could say that it wasn't his own money, and we'd have to admit that the accounting system in Shahbaddin left a lot to be desired in the 1910s. Nevertheless, the presumptions would be with us. They'd have to break them to succeed.'

'You must be spending a lot of money,' she said at once.

'Not to worry about the money.'

'But I do. I think Sir John spoke of cash in a bank. As well as the trust and house, I mean.'

'There are two thousand pounds in a current account.'

'And does the injunction cover that?'

'Most certainly not.'

'Then could you draw it out for me?'

'Yes, but it isn't necessary. We're acting for you as executrix.' He coughed a professional cough. 'You'll be getting a bill in the end.'

'I hate running into debt,' she said. 'It isn't lawful.'

'Lawful?' He sounded puzzled.

'I mean it isn't favoured by the religion I was brought up in.'

'And not much by mine.'

'I know.'

She laughed as she shook hands and he showed her out. They went down in the lift and into the little courtyard. He found her a taxi.

Back at his desk he rubbed his hands. It was a habit he deplored and had nearly broken, but in moments of emotion caught him out. He was now in extreme emotion. . . . What a woman, what a lifetime's lay! Of course it was mad to think of it but he was thinking of it powerfully. And the file had mentioned casually that she might have an understanding with Geoffrey Addis, old Clement's son. But knowing Geoffrey Addis, looking at Sheila Raden, Marks's inclination had been to doubt it. There'd been nothing in *The Times* and she wore no ring; she hadn't the air of a girl bespoken. Geoffrey Addis, heir to Mastertons, Court Jewellers and all that.

David Marks snorted. He had met Geoffrey Addis and thought nothing of him at all. He had the tolerance of his people but also its quick contempt for a mug. Not that Geoffrey was a mug, he was shrewder than most. He was a gentleman in superior trade, perhaps a little too conscious that the former could be important. Wine-merchants, family jewellers. . . .

They were most of them stuffed shirts.

David Marks blew his nose but he didn't cool quickly. He despised Geoffrey Addis but his instincts went deeper. He hated waste and this was waste intolerable. Some inhibited Christian would crawl into that gorgeous bed, a hand where he'd put his own soft mouth, a knee where he'd put a tormenting hand. . . .

David Marks choked but he swallowed it down. He began to swear disgracefully.

The man they called Oliver Kendry was very tired. He felt this now almost more than the incessant pain. He'd been in very great pain for ninety-six hours, varied by moments of intolerable agony.

He hadn't expected it, he'd been totally unprepared. He was

a shy man with something of the scholar's detachment, deliberately uninterested in politics. His mother, already a widow, had died when he'd been only a boy, and he'd been educated in England by his uncle, Sir Montagu Raden. But not at a public school. Oliver Kendry's blood was half Malay, and Sir Montagu had been too sensitive to expose it to the rigours of an English boy-factory. The family house in Hampshire was staffed only for the shooting, but there'd been a cottage as a dower house and Oliver Kendry had come to manhood there with tutors. The tutors had been good ones, he hadn't been forced in any way, but he'd had a natural bent for learning. He had gone to Cambridge happily when the tutors had been outgrown, relaxed and entirely comfortable in its easy all-races tolerance. He was decently provided for but had been taught to eschew mere idleness, and back in Shahbaddin again he ran the capital's public library.

He knew that the state was disturbed and restless, and he'd been taught with his mother's milk to mistrust Chinese, but he'd always kept out of politics, partly from inclination, partly because, though he called himself Oliver Kendry, everyone who mattered knew he was really Oliver Raden. And Radens no longer ruled. He wouldn't himself have wished to rule even if he'd had title to.

A quiet man living quietly.

He'd been shutting up the library when the three Chinese had come storming in. They beat him half-senseless brutally, then bundled him at gunpoint into the black saloon outside. There they blindfolded him and bound him, and he thought they had driven for maybe an hour. Then they'd thrown him into this windowless room, and here he had been for he thought four days. He wasn't quite sure for he couldn't see the sun. In any case light was something to fear since light meant more torture. *Them.* Time had begun to slip, his own mind with it. It had been worse than any Christian's hell.

At first he'd been simply outraged. . . . The gold, they'd said, we've got to have the gold. Half dizzy from the beating still he'd stared at them uncomprehendingly. . . . What gold?

Your uncle's gold, the gold he stole from the people he was supposed to love.

'I didn't know he had any.'

They had laughed but not for long.

He'd protested of course, but they hadn't listened; he'd sworn on his father's grave but they still went on. In the darkness he shivered. They'd taken his watch but a timeless internal clock still ran. It was telling him that in an hour at most the agony would start again.

He began to weep weakly but unashamed. The horror was that he knew nothing at all: this might go on for weeks and months. They thought he was being stubborn but he couldn't have stood it a minute if he'd had knowledge. He had prayed to his God for death but his God had gone. And their professionalism was the worst of all—unbearable. They didn't appear to enjoy it but they were utterly without pity. His screams they ignored, his vomitings avoided. When he fainted they brought him back to this sunless room. For a moment consciousness left him for the bliss of an exhausted doze.

He was woken from it by gunfire, first single shots, then the chatter of a machine-gun. He listened with near indifference, his mind not grooving. There was another burst from an automatic weapon, then silence for several minutes. A knock on the door.

He shivered again. They'd never knocked.

'Mr Kendry? Are you inside?'

He didn't dare answer.

The man outside the door began to talk in Malay. 'Keep away from the door. We're blowing it.'

There was a blistering crack of fire against the lock. The light had come on from the switch outside and Oliver saw splinters flying. An oath and another burst. Then the lock began to teeter. It fell finally, deliberately, a tinkle on the cold stone floor. The door opened and a man came in, walking almost diffidently. He had a machine-pistol slung on a canvas sling and a tiny wisp of acid smoke curled greyly from its muzzle.

. . . Power grows out of the end of a gun.

He was a thickset Malay, tense but moving smoothly. He held out his hand; saw Oliver's; withdrew it. Instead he said simply:

'Come with us.'

The next twenty-four hours were an almost total blank to him, but Oliver Raden could remember another car. Then a bungalow in the foothills, a doctor for his broken hands, and food and sleep. Even a bath though he'd had to wear rubber gloves for it. It was all very kind but it was also very hurried: These men knew their purpose but for the moment they weren't telling it.

They told him next morning when an older man came to his room. He was a Malay again but they spoke in English. He addressed a shattered Kendry as Mr Raden, and clearly it wasn't a slip of the tongue. He put a passport in Oliver's better hand and Oliver glanced down at it. It was his own in the name of Kendry.

'They call me simply Sayed and in English that's more than enough. I'm sorry to seem discourteous but we simply haven't time to explain. That will come in London where you'll be met at Heathrow tomorrow night.' The older man smiled. 'By a member of our brotherhood.'

Oliver managed to say: 'I see.'

'I rather doubt it, Mr Raden, but very soon you will. We've a passage on an aircraft and we're prepared to see it takes you.' The older man smiled again, this time a different smile. 'Oh yes,' he said, 'we can guarantee that much.'

'If you could tell me what's happening——'

'I can tell you what's happened. You were taken by Chinese agents and tortured for the Raden gold.'

'I was tortured all right. . . . What Raden gold?'

'I know no more than you do—yet.' Sayed spoke politely but was suddenly very serious. 'But I do know your real name's Raden.' He looked at Oliver appraisingly. 'I'm inclined to think that's a good enough reason.'

'For sending me to London?'

'No. Inviting you.'

Oliver Raden considered it. He wasn't, he knew, in adequate shape for considering, but what was left of his hands had started to twitch again. He heard himself say:

'I'll go.'

The man they called Sayed spoke Malay as he answered. 'May Allah protect your flight,' he said.

CHAPTER TWO

In his room above Mastertons Clement Addis was thinking. The firm was a family business still, Clement the third Addis to head it. It was studiously old-fashioned and its clientele unflashy, but many of them were very rich and some of these rich still British. There'd be one or two things in the window and they'd be superlative of their kind. Above the plate glass the Royal Warrant glowed discreetly, splendidly emblazoned, heraldically correct for once. It had cost Clement's grandfather a hundred guineas. The street was quiet but in the heart of West One. Buses didn't run in it for these were the shops of the custom trade. When you'd finished your business a commissionaire found you a taxi.

Clement Addis was a beautifully dressed man of seventy, Old Clement Addis. He knew that he was called that now, but well into his sixties and the adjective would have been quite misplaced. He was still trim and active, but now old age had snatched at his sleeve, old age in the person of Dorothy Addis. He had married her in his sixties when Dorothy had been twenty-five, a year younger than his own son had been, the Geoffrey Addis who would succeed him. If, that is, there was very much left to succeed to. Business hadn't been going so well and nor had his private life. His wide mouth closed stubbornly for he was conscious of a mistake. Everyone who had dared to, everyone with any claim, had told him or hinted the same drear thing: Dorothy was twenty-five, he just in his sixties. He was a foolish old man and you always paid.

Just the same he had married her.

And now he was seventy, Dorothy Addis a well-kept thirty-three. The hour and the day had arrived inevitably, not with anger or sensationally, but for reasons he'd always known would come. So he didn't wish to divorce her, she didn't wish to remarry. She was, he reflected coolly, very well as she was. No doubt she had a lover but she was much too clever to flaunt him. The situation was being managed well, handled as he would have wished to—the home out of London, the discreet flat in town. Clement Addis had a door key but he telephoned before using it. This was really nothing new to him, only his own part in it, and he'd certainly had his second youth. They couldn't take that away from him and he'd always expected to pay for it.

But not quite so much, not quite so brutally. For Dorothy was a spendthrift who was bleeding Clement Addis white. For all his worldly wisdom he hadn't spotted the killer trait.

He put Dorothy behind him since he had troubles more immediate. This ridiculous injunction—he'd been astonished and contemptuous. All Orientals were crazy. The crown jewels of the kingdom—the idea was a fantasy. The Radens weren't the sort to own crown jewels. They'd had a private safe in Mastertons for more years than he cared to think about, by no means the only family which did so. Clement Addis had been ready to swear formally to its contents. There was a good deal of family junk, but one good piece, something Sir Montagu Raden, Bart, had ironically called 'the coronet'. But Clement's lawyers had advised him that an affidavit wouldn't be adequate. The High Commissioner was pressing and he should offer an undertaking that the safe's contents would not be touched. The real case would be fixed for an early date, and then they could fight it out in court, title to whatever the safe contained. Addis had nothing to gain and a lot to lose, a lot to lose if he too openly took sides.

He knew that the advice was good but it had also been distasteful. For his instincts had been to take sides sharply. Montagu Raden had been his friend, he'd dined with him and shot in Hampshire, and now he was one of his daughter's trustees. Sheila Raden, a great beauty, and his son wished to marry her.

He turned his thoughts to Geoffrey Addis, reluctantly since

he wasn't sure. He was his only child, the son of his first wife, born rather late in a flawless marriage. There'd been another wife in legitimate line between Geoffrey's mother and Dorothy Addis, for Clement who loved women had also been contemptuous of what he thought of as mere liaisons. They offended his sense of dignity. Now, a full and vigorous life behind him, he was considering Geoffrey, his only son.

He wasn't sure, he really wasn't. The boy had been a model son, not the sort to give a father a moment's worry. No guitars, no left-wing period, National Service as a Rifleman, his father's club as a matter of course. He was competent in the business, too, and had brought in new custom discreetly. It was a finely conventional record and to old Clement rather a dull one. What did Geoffrey do about women, come to that? His father didn't know but suspected nothing. That mightn't be quite incredible but it wasn't a recommendation. Not when you were courting Sheila Raden.

The old man smiled his gentle satyr's smile. He'd met the girl often from childhood on; her blazing beauty could still stir him as it would stir any man who was one. Geoffrey Addis, for instance—whatever he was he wasn't bent. That mightn't be enough though, and in Clement's view would not be. She might have him or she might turn him down and the old man wouldn't have bet on it, but if she took him that wouldn't end it. No. He'd still have to hold her and he might not carry the guns.

His father, a little ashamed, was almost certain that he didn't. He wasn't a strange one, by no means that: the wife of Geoffrey Addis wouldn't simply be a cover girl. But he was terribly, well, say English. There was nothing against that of course, the fashion for praising foreigners was being heavily overplayed. In any case it was irrelevant. What mattered was Sheila Raden and she was very much a woman. The old man knew, for he'd married three. Better that than a dozen mistresses. Marrying them you learnt, you really did.

His secretary brought in tea and he looked at his neat

diary. There was nothing of great importance today but there was an awkward affair tomorrow.

'This man from the High Commissioner's is coming to-morrow morning?'

'Yes, at noon.'

'Please ask Mr Geoffrey if he'll take him in my place.'

He had spoken on an impulse but he didn't withdraw the words. The interview would be tiresome and it would be very good practice for Geoffrey. One half of Clement Addis nodded approvingly—there was nothing like letting a crown prince work; the other half knew he was ducking out. The interview would be troublesome, some tedious Oriental, blustering first, they always did, then probably trying to bribe him. Delicately at first, then producing a cheque-book or even cash, trying to get a peep into the safe before the case came on. The contemporary orthodoxy was that they were just as good as you were. Maybe—he wouldn't deny it. But they were just as good in a different way and Clement Addis was seventy.

The old man sighed for he was cheating himself and knew it. Five years ago and he'd have positively relished it, the half-truths, the cut and thrust, the clash of wills. Experience for Geoffrey? Alas, that was self-deception. It was a great deal simpler than that and a lot less happy.

It was hell growing old.

Sheila Raden was dining with Geoffrey Addis, watching him talk to the wine-waiter. She wasn't permitted to drink herself but insisted that others who wanted to should. Her father had always done that and so did she. She was amused but concealed it. What Geoffrey would be drinking would probably be potable but it wouldn't be worth this learned fuss with a wine-waiter hiding his boredom. He'd have heard it all before but he'd play along. That was part of his job but the part he liked least.

When he'd finished with the winemanship Geoffrey Addis began to talk. He talked well, she thought, but only up to a certain point. Push him beyond and he'd simply stare, clam up. She knew because she'd tried it. She was quite without malice but she was a woman and liked to tease. Geoffrey was saying easily:

'Things in Shahbaddin seem to have got in a bit of a mess.'

'They've been messy for years.'

'I meant this evening's news.'

'I haven't seen the evening paper. As a matter of fact I don't go much for newspapers. I read a weekly at week ends and I read it pretty thoroughly. And that's about the lot.'

'Which one?'

She told him.

'But that's very left wing.' He sounded surprised and she could sense he was disapproving.

'Don't get me wrong. I don't accept the weekly dose as something out of holy writ. When it comes to hard news my weekly simply doesn't rate, and it always gets hold of the wrong end of the stick. That's why I read it—I can often guess the right one.'

'It's an original approach,' he said. He took her at her literal word since he hadn't a great deal of humour. He was thinking that she was pretty quick and he knew she'd been sensibly educated. Sir Montagu Raden had chosen carefully, and Geoffrey Addis approved his choice. He hadn't packed her off to England to some fashionable ladies' prison but had made his little arrangement with the Reverend Mother locally. A Moslem girl in a Catholic school had sounded a total nonsense, but Geoffrey had Catholic cousins and he knew that it was not. The form was as fixed as the Faith itself and the Reverend Mother would follow it. She'd have a duty in religion which was bluntly to make converts, and if she didn't remember, her confessor would remind her. But the Reverend Mother had been an aristocratic Frenchwoman and she wouldn't take orders easily from some half-educated Irish peasant because he happened to be a priest. Instead she'd play it both ways and in fact had done just that, delicately contriving that Sheila should know what the true faith offered, then, when she wasn't interested, withdrawing just as delicately. After all the girl was a Moslem, Islam a perfectly respectable revealed religion. It was mistaken no doubt, but it was anything but contemptible. It wasn't as though the girl were a damned Protestant.

Geoffrey was rolling his wine round judicially. 'This isn't bad.'

'I'm glad.'

He put down his glass. 'Going back to Shahbaddin again, there was a pretty big riot there yesterday.'

'What sort of a riot?'

'Is there more than one sort in Shahbaddin?'

'Of course there is.' He'd annoyed her but didn't notice. 'It looked like Malays against Chinese.'

'Trying to burn down the Chinese shops?'

He nodded. 'I think so.'

'Then the best of British luck to them.'

He asked a little uncertainly: 'You don't like the Chinese?'

'That's far too simple. You've got to remember that apart from holidays in Hampshire I've spent most of my life in Shahbaddin. I've absorbed the local prejudices and I happen to be a Moslem.'

'Yes,' he said, 'I know.'

He knew, she thought, but did he care? She hadn't an inkling. If she took him, would he expect her to turn Christian? An Englishman would be capable of it. He hadn't yet asked her but she was certain that he would do so. But he was a conventional man, he was taking his time; he was going through the motions as they'd taught him in the army.

She would have liked to smile but didn't. Instead she asked: 'Our case comes up next week, I think?'

'It does, thank the Lord. It's a load of rubbish. How they can possibly talk that nonsense about crown jewels——'

'That government will say anything.'

'You don't like them either?'

Again she avoided it. 'I didn't say that.' He might misunderstand her or more likely he wouldn't, but if she was going to accept him, even to go on seeing him, she had to put the record straight. 'I'm a Moslem,' she said again, 'and so are the Malays. But there are Chinese in the government too and Chinese are simply heathens——'

'Like me,' he said surprisingly.

'——but they've been there a very long time, they've a right to live. So as long as it keeps a balance between the two I'm for any sort of government which can make the country tick. But you know about Chinese—they're like the Jews. They can do anything in this world except behave with moderation.'

He changed the subject and she was glad of it. 'What will you do with your father's house?'

'I'll sell it if I can but I'll keep the cottage.'

'It might pay you to keep the whole thing and let the shooting.'

'I might do that if I have to. If I've got it still in October will your father be taking a gun again?'

'I'm afraid he won't.' Geoffrey added in apology: 'He's getting past shooting.'

There was a note in his voice which caught her ear. Clement Addis had two passions and the second of them was shooting. He'd taken a gun last year and shot well. Why, he didn't even wear glasses to shoot. It would need something more than a twinge of age to keep Clement away from Averley.

She knew little of business, had no taste for affairs, but when you came to think of it the Addises weren't really rich. They were comfortable and maybe more, but a superior jewellers could hardly be a gold-mine—not today. She looked at Geoffrey Addis under the sweep of luxuriant eyelashes. She had two thousand a year from a trust and a house to sell, and there was some jewellery in a safe worth she didn't know what. Very probably less than she'd ever guess, but there was one good piece, for she'd seen her mother wear it. Hell, she was an heiress.

She almost laughed as the pompous word struck her, but you didn't laugh with Geoffrey around if you weren't prepared to explain the joke. He was eating, head down, and she looked at him again. Would he be courting her for her money? No, do him justice, he probably wouldn't do that, but do him justice again, a different sort, and he'd have heard the ancient saw. Never marry for money, but marry where money is. After all, she thought quite innocently, he was really middle-class.

When they had finished leisurely Geoffrey Addis found a taxi. He handed her in and for a second seemed to hesitate. Then he climbed in beside her. She knew what was coming and it might or might not be interesting. He took her hand first, then, when she didn't snatch it, kissed her.

Sheila hadn't a woman crony, much preferring men to natter to, but if she'd had such a thing she'd have told her the truth. She'd been kissing in a taxi. Naturally not for the first time but this young man had been serious. He was perfectly respect-able, even rather handsome in his stifled English way. And it might have been her brother. She hadn't giggled but had wanted to.

At her flat he paid the taxi and stood on the pavement, silent. He waited for a moment but she didn't ask him in. Nor did he invite himself. At last he waved and walked away.

She went slowly up the staircase with a thought which had astonished her. She was thinking of David Marks and not unkindly. With David it wouldn't have gone like that. Quite to the contrary. He'd have pushed her into a taxi, probably choosing a driver of his own race. Then he'd have shut all the windows and most likely tried to rape her. That mightn't have been agreeable, no, but it wouldn't have been a giggle.

At the door of her duplex she felt in her bag for the key. It wasn't there. She was careless of trifles and her carelessness annoyed her. Now she'd have to wake the housekeeper and the lady wouldn't be pleased at all. Unless, that is, she'd been doubly careless, both forgetting her key and leaving the latch off. She turned the handle tentatively, and the polished door opened.

A man was sitting quietly in an old-fashioned chintz arm-chair. For a moment she thought of burglars, but he'd turned on a light and as he rose she saw his face. He came to the door and took her hand. 'Cousin,' he said, and kissed it.

She noticed at once he was still wearing gloves.

Geoffrey Addis was in his father's room, waiting for his caller from the High Commissioner's office. He'd been given his style and title, which seemed to consist of the names of old Moslem dignitaries liberally sprinkled with the derivative *bins*. Geoffrey had been practising it, mildly confident that he could manage the alien sounds or something like them. He was astonished when a Chinese walked in. His secretary gallantly tried his name. It sounded like Uhlan King but couldn't be that. The Chinese smiled pleasantly. 'Just call me Mr Kin,' he said. He spoke excellent English with a powerful Brooklyn accent.

'Please sit down, Mr Kin.'

The Chinese did so. 'I should explain my presence. My colleague who was coming has eaten something which disagreed with him.' The accent was Brooklyn, the idiom emphatically not.

'I'm sorry.'

'It's nothing, I assure you. And I'm sure we can do business.'

'If it's about that injunction——'

'It is. You'll have heard, of course, that the case has been postponed.'

Geoffrey hadn't and said so. This could hardly be a lie.

'The law's delays are entirely scandalous. We only heard ourselves last night.'

It was true, Kin was thinking, but it wasn't all that important. He'd have had to come here anyway or pursue an expensive lawsuit which he'd always considered unhelpful to his real purpose. His High Commissioner knew that aim but was embarrassed by it and frightened, so a lawsuit had been the compromise, the High Commissioner's after reference home. And the Legal Adviser had said the same. Kin despised the pair of them, for one was an English hireling, the other a venal Malay by now so near to a terrified switch of loyalties that he could soon be quite ignored. But perhaps not just yet. The crown jewels of the kingdom. . . .

They could have the crown jewels—very probably there weren't any. Kin had much larger game in his sights, the matter of the Raden gold, and secret and urgent instructions which the High Commissioner knew nothing about. Meanwhile he had better be sure about the contents of that troublesome safe.

Geoffrey Addis was asking: 'But what's happened about the case?'

'The judge, like my colleague, has gone sick. Nothing serious again, just some tiresome judicial sniffle. We might get the case heard in another court but that could mean as much delay as waiting for his lordship to recover.'

'How much delay?'

'They thought about a fortnight.' Kin had been lolling but now sat up suddenly. 'You can see this changes everything.'

'I don't quite see how.'

'We can't wait too long. For knowledge—for certainty.'

'I'm not sure I follow you.'

The Chinese said patiently: 'Oh come, Mr Addis, we're men of the world. Let me recap on the events. My government is claiming that you're holding assets which belong to it, not to the client who rents your safe. We've good reason to believe that this property's very valuable or we wouldn't have taken the gamble of litigation.' His voice went up a half-tone. 'We've got to know what that propery is. And soon.'

'My father offered a sworn list, you know.' He was temporizing instinctively.

'Mr Addis, you embarrass me.' Kin sounded genuinely embarrassed. 'Put yourself in my position as I'll try to put myself in yours. You're one of the most eminent jewellers in London but I represent a government. Suppose I sent a signal home that we'd accepted an affidavit. How long do you think I should last *en poste*?'

Geoffrey didn't answer since he didn't have a good one.

'You take my point? But of course you do. We were content

with an injunction when the matter was coming to court in days. There'd have been an order for inspection and if the safe had just held rubbish we'd have certainly dropped the case. We'd have preferred something quicker but we could live with a few days.'

'But you said only a fortnight longer still.'

'Unacceptable. There are reasons. Reasons of state.'

. . . Here it comes.

'So I'm asking you to help us.'

'Yes?'

'I want a look at that safe—no more. You have my word——'

Geoffrey said promptly: 'Impossible. There's an injunction which runs till the court decides what to do.'

'I don't think you quite realize how we stand.' The other's manner had slightly changed. It wasn't the bluster old Addis had expected but the air of a man who held a fair hand and knew it. 'My government is seeking property which it genuinely believes belongs to it. We're entitled to help and officially we've asked for it. We feel we're entitled to your private co-operation too.'

'We can't possibly do what you ask, you must know that.'

The Chinese said softly: 'If we went to the authorities again, a government they're rather anxious to oblige . . . Mastertons obstructing us . . .'

'The authorities would know the law.'

'They also know many people. Rich ones—your clients.'

'Mr Kin, are you threatening me?' Geoffrey was very formal. He could be formal when he wished to and too often when he did not.

The other ignored it. 'Then you won't do business?'

'I can't.'

'Mr Addis, you're misunderstanding again. The word I'm now stressing is business, not your help.'

. . . Now it's down to the straight lolly. A cheque perhaps, or more likely cash. It was a mistake to suppose that Orientals were always delicate.

34

Mr Kin held a briefcase and now opened it deliberately. He didn't let Geoffrey see inside but he put on his desk a neat bundle of notes. They were tenners, the pile substantial. Geoffrey guessed it at a thousand pounds.

Mr Kin didn't speak but looked at Geoffrey. Geoffrey was looking away from the notes.

The Chinese produced another bundle. Geoffrey played with a cigarette. A pause. Another bundle. Mr Kin said quietly, finally: 'And that's my limit.'

Geoffrey Addis was excited but not by greed. . . . Three grand—this must be serious. He rose and walked to the door, holding it open. Mr Kin rose too and followed him. The money was still on the desk where Kin had left it. Geoffrey said icily:

'I think you've forgotten something.'

The Chinese shrugged and recovered the money. He came back to the door and now he wasn't smiling. As he went past Geoffrey he said softly:

'I don't think you quite realize just how serious this could be. For all of us.'

Charles Russell was talking to his Minister on the telephone in his flat. It was a security telephone and they were speaking quite freely. Harry Tuke was saying crisply:

'You remember we were talking in my club? The day you were too amiable to show me how bad the meal was.'

Russell looked at the clock: it was coming up for midnight. Harry Tuke would not be drunk but he'd have taken drink judiciously.

'Yes, I remember.'

'Shahbaddin, to remind you. You were full of wise saws about Shahbaddin.' Tuke mimicked Charles Russell's voice; he did it unmaliciously but evidently relishing it. ' "There was some sort of bastard nephew, I hear, but he wasn't interested in politics. Anyway, he wasn't recognized." '

'I said something like that.'

35

'Well, he's now turned up in England. He landed at Heathrow last night.'

'How do you know?'

'One of our officials out there was flying home on leave. The same aircraft and he saw him.'

'And what's that to us?'

'Charles, I'm not fooling, I explained the position.' There was a well-timed and effective pause. 'If that government breaks, the Chinks are in.'

'But why should it break down because this man's come to London?'

'But I told you. If we're to keep the Chinese out of Shahbaddin we've got to shore up the present lot, and they'll collapse like straw if they think that we're letting them down. In particular letting them down on the Raden jewellery. They're seeing that as a clear test case of what our support is really worth. So this Raden flies suddenly to London, where the family baubles are already much hotter than we should like them——'

'Aren't you guessing his intentions a trifle fast?'

'I hope so—my God, I hope so. And there's another thing too. He was met at the airport. The official noticed that too.'

'By whom?'

'By a Malay.'

'Is that supposed to be sinister?'

'I wish I knew.'

Charles Russell said resignedly: 'Then what do you want me to do?'

'Your stuff.'

'All right, I'll keep an eye on him. For what that's worth in a case like this and that's probably nothing at all.'

CHAPTER THREE

Sheila was watching Oliver Raden drink the China tea with lemon which she had made him. She hadn't seen him for three years but he didn't seem to have changed much. He was thinner than she remembered, but he'd always been slim, even tall for a man of mixed blood. He held himself well when he remembered to, but had a hint of the scholar's stoop when he did not. His face showed almost nothing of varied ancestry, a hint about the eyes perhaps, the hairline a fraction lower than Sheila's own. He wore his short hair *en brosse*, and it sprang from his scalp with a vigorous masculinity. He was bronzed without trace of sallowness and his dark eyes, though shocked, were alert and humorous. He might have been a Frenchman from the Midi. He was saying conversationally:

'It is kind of you to receive me. I hope you do not mind that I just walked in.' He smiled, showing beautiful teeth. 'I found the door open.'

He spoke English without an accent, or if there was one it was Cambridge, but gave an unmistakable impression that he didn't think in it or dream. It was correct but a trifle careful, a contrast to the quick give-and-take of Sheila's own friends and contemporaries. Not, she thought quickly, that she should class him in a different age. There were fourteen years between them and when she'd been a child still it had seemed like a lifetime. Now she was a woman it was nothing. He'd be thirty-six or thirty-seven, only a few years older than Geoffrey Addis.

Whom she didn't now wish to think about since Oliver was more interesting.

They'd always been on easy terms and she could ask him without offence: 'Would you rather talk Malay?' She was perfectly bilingual as the Radens had been for a century. 'Just till the English comes back a bit.'

'That's really very thoughtful of you. I'm a little out of practice with the language of my father. I read in it all day, but there aren't many people to whom to talk it.'

'Not that terrible English colony—no. All right, let's talk Malay.'

They laughed together, relaxed at once.

She nodded at his still gloved hands. 'But have you had an accident?'

'A sort of accident.'

There was something in his voice which made her stare, a note of uncertainty, of feeling his way. This wasn't his normal manner and Sheila was promptly curious.

'But you don't work with your hands.'

'No, I suppose I don't.'

'Come on,' she said, 'tell me.'

He looked at her for some time. 'If I tell you it may start something.'

'London isn't that exciting.' She was something more than curious now.

'I don't work with my hands but somebody worked on them.'

'Stop talking in riddles.'

'I was tortured,' he said. He didn't want her pity, he feared her tears. She gave him neither, flaring instead in an instant rage.

'Who tortured you?'

'Some Chinese thugs. I'd never seen them before and they didn't talk like locals.'

'They tortured a Raden.' She could hardly get the words out.

'I'm a Kendry on my passport.'

'Like hell you're a Kendry, like hell you're the butler's son. You're Oliver Raden to me and always were.'

For a moment she thought he was going to weep. 'You wouldn't say that if you knew what I did.'

'Why ever not?'

'I screamed,' he said. 'I screamed and screamed.'

'Of course you did, who wouldn't?'

'Your father wouldn't have screamed, or mine.'

'Phooey.' Her annoyance reassured him as no sympathy ever could have. 'What terrible tripe you're talking.' Her casual matter-of-factness was more convincing than any protest. To give herself time to think she said: 'I'll make us some fresh tea.

She went into the kitchenette, using the moment to clear her mind. When she'd been younger she'd sometimes wondered, asking herself why her uncle had never married this slim man's mother. She'd been a gentle, charming woman, much more than just a mistress but a fit consort for a Raden. But later Sheila had realized that the reason lay in that single word. No Raden would care tuppence for the middle-class disapproval of the race-conscious British colony, but Oliver's father had expected to inherit and the Radens had survived for a hundred years by observing a simple but basic rule. They had held the scales scrupulously, utterly impartial between Chinese and Malay. They were impartial and were seen to be. But take a wife from one race, present to the other an heir half-committed . . .

Their position could have crumbled in a year. Of course it had crumbled anyway now, but Oliver's father had been heir-apparent and he'd known what was owed to a hundred years. Nor would an acknowledged bastard have been politically acceptable. So poor daddy Kendry, the butler who'd bought it. He'd been an amiable old gentleman, an excellent servant if a little too fond of the bottle. He hadn't, at his age, been interested in women, but he'd been perfectly willing to lend his name, even a little flattered. Oliver had been in and out all day, as acceptable in her grandfather's house as she herself had accepted him. He'd been too old to share her nursery but that was a difference of age alone. She'd been telling the simple truth when she'd said he was Oliver Raden. To Sheila he'd never been anything else.

She had gone to the kitchen as much to collect herself as to set up another tea-tray, but now she'd recovered she took the tray back to the living-room. Oliver was sitting still, smoking a pale Dutch cheroot.

'Do you mind the smoke?'

'Of course not.'

It was pleasing him to make small talk but he'd tell her everything in time. He always had. It would be maladroit to rush him, but one thing she must be sure of.

'You said it was Chinese who tortured you?' She reinforced the substantive with a salty doric adjective, a word he hadn't known she knew.

He showed his splendid teeth again. 'Your Malay's still pretty good,' he said.

'Don't duck me, I won't take it.'

'Yes, it was Chinese did it.'

'But why?'

'I'm not quite sure I know that yet.'

She was annoyed again but hid it. 'And you haven't even told me why you're in England.'

'I'm not sure I know that either.'

She started to speak but he held up a hand. A little surprised she found she'd stopped dead. Oliver looked at his watch.

'There's a late programme on TV tonight, I think they call it *Worldline*. There's been trouble in Shahbaddin again and they might have something on it. I'd like to watch.'

She shrugged and turned the set on. The voice came first, smooth and oleaginous. 'Tonight the *Worldline* team is taking you to Shahbaddin. Not all of you will have heard of it. . . ."

. . . That's a really slippery statement. One in fifty will know the place exists, the rest won't care.

'. . . but Shabaddin is racked by rioting, a disturbance of a fierceness it has never known before.'

The picture had come up at last, the self-important be-spectacled face, the hair which could do with a wash, the air of uneasy omniscience.

'I detest that man, he gives me the creeps.'

'Be quiet, girl,' Oliver Raden said. 'Be silent.' He had spoken

40

in English and she stared at him, astonished. She opened her mouth to protest but it didn't come.

The beefy British Inspector of Police was thoroughly unhappy. He'd drunk two pints of beer at lunch and had expected to get his feet up. In the afternoons he mostly did, and with a temperature in the damp nineties the habit was both necessary and civilized.

But not this afternoon. It had started in the normal way, an almost routine scuffle on the fringe of the Chinese quarter. The Inspector had sent a sergeant and dozed, but his telephone had rung at once. This wasn't a routine scuffle but a crowd of perhaps ten thousand. And it was growing every minute. The Inspector had cursed, but had called his car.

Now, the beer sour in his stomach, he was standing in it watching, and for the past half-hour he'd been constantly on his radio. His Superintendent would be arriving soon with the last of the men he could manage to lay his hands on.

For this was serious—not the least doubt of it. The Inspector had seen nothing like it in his considerable service. He was looking down the street into the square. It was solid with shouting men and still they came. In the centre was a bedraggled garden, a broken fountain and dusty trees. The Inspector, who was experienced, frowned. In any small disturbance the trees would be black with urchins watching the fun. There wasn't, this afternoon, a child in sight.

But he knew his job and what he must do. Four streets led into the square and he was blocking the northern. He hadn't the men to block the rest, the funnels which fed the swelling crowd, but he could block the northern street and must. He must because it was straight and wide, the only artery into the heart of the Chinese quarter.

God rot those damned Chinese, he thought. They often seemed to ask for it and today they quite clearly had.

He knew what he must do but he was out of his depth emotionally. He'd seen plenty of disturbances but this one frankly scared him. Normally a crowd would chant:

41

'Down with the Chinese pigs' or 'Death to the unbelievers,' ancestral slogans of vulgar hate which few took wholly seriously and those that did would soon forget. But today the cries were different, a rhythmic 'Shahbaddin' and nothing more. 'Shahbaddin, Shahbaddin.' He'd never heard that cry before nor thought he would live to hear it.

In the sweltering heat he shivered for he was wise in the ways of crowds. If its note went down a half-tone he'd be in very serious trouble.

But he had made his dispositions and reviewed them now professionally. Across the entrance to the vital street stretched the portable barriers the police kept in lorries, wire on cross-posts of wood, the feet of the crosses anchored by concrete blocks. It was enough to control a crowd and always had, but it couldn't be guaranteed to hold determined men in riot.

'They're pressing up pretty close to the wire.' He was talking to his sergeant.

'They can't help it with that crowd behind, the square's filling every second.'

. . . And those behind cried forward while those behind cried back. That was something they'd made him learn at school, some classy old Roman defending a bridge. Well, he wasn't a classy Roman but he was certainly defending. And another thing, there were knives out now. He'd seen more than one flash in the merciless sun. The crowd was up against the wire.

The sergeant had a loudhailer out. 'Stand away. Get back.'

They did not move.

'I don't think they'll try to pull it down. Not yet. But if that square gets any fuller the thing'll just go by pressure."

'Then we'll have to give them a whiff of gas.'

There was the hollow plop of the rifle grenades as the gas went away in canisters. They'd been aimed at the first six ranks of the crowd, breaking on impact with bodies packed solid, the pale smoke curling wispily. There was cursing and coughing and perhaps ten feet gained.

'Poor bastards, they'd like to break. They can't.'

'But they are,' the Inspector said. 'They are.' He didn't believe his eyes nor wish to.

In the centre, incredibly, the crowd was somehow parting. An ancient car, its radiator steaming, was forcing a passage through them.

'They must be mad,' the sergeant said.

'They're not.' The Inspector pointed.

The broken-down clanking car had a shield in front, two sheets of iron lashed with rope in a pointed V.

The sergeant said incredulously: 'My God, it's going to charge us.'

The Inspector stood silent, hesitating. He was a kindly man, he hated bloodshed; he also had his duty and his pride. He said at last almost bitterly: "Fire. Don't brown the crowd but stop that car.'

There was a volley from kneeling Malay police but the marksmanship wasn't notable. In the back of the car a standing man dropped but another pulled him out and took his place.

The car came on.

The Inspector said reluctantly: 'Give me a rifle.' A constable passed him his weapon and he looked at it reflectively. It wasn't an impressive piece. The Inspector worked the bolt five times, emptying the rifle of the ball cartridge in the magazine. Then he pulled from his pocket a single and lethal pointed round. He took deliberate aim and shot the driver.

The man at the driver's side hardly glanced at the body. He pulled it down to the floor and took its place, all in a single smooth movement. The car was clear of the crowd at last and had ten feet left to accelerate. The new driver used them.

The Inspector was reloading but he didn't have time to fire again. There was a grinding crash and the car was through. Four or five men jumped out but the police were firing grimly now. Three of the car's crew went down and one got up unsteadily. The crowd had begun to chant again and the Inspector listened carefully. There was a roar of rage, then a second of silence. Then the noise the Inspector feared worse than death, the low-pitched growl of a crowd turned riot.

43

They were coming through the barrier now, water released from a broken dam. The Inspector had his revolver out but a native knife took most of his hand off. He stood stupidly watching the bleeding stump. But not for long. He felt another knife in his lower ribs, then a wound in his neck and another. He fell and kicked twice in the arid dust.

On the roof of a building ten yards up the street a cameraman was being sick, and sixty hours later the switchboard at the B.B.C. was jammed with protesting callers.

The B.B.C. had expected that. It was the only adult programme of the week.

The scene faded out and the self-satisfied spectacled face came back, the carefully classless voice. That Man. Sheila Raden got up and switched him off. In several million homes there was a similar click. The action, what was interesting, was over.

'Thank you for showing me that,' she said. 'I'm beginning to understand.'

But he shook his head. 'I'm afraid it isn't as simple as it seems. I wish it were. We've had riots before and we'll have them again. I've seen several and I can smell if they're serious. The standard form is for a Chinese to swindle some poor Malay, then the latter calls his neighbours and they try to sack the Chinese shop. Sometimes a single policeman can handle it, less often it spreads and they have to use a squad of them.' He nodded at the now dark screen. 'But what we've just been looking at had something I've never seen before, a sort of, well, *desperation*. And I've never before seen a policeman killed.'

'I agree it didn't look normal, and you're perfectly right, there *was* something. But I've been away here three years——'

'You'd like me to bring you up to date?'

'Yes please.'

He began to tick it off quickly. 'It started when the British tried to ease out your father, and from where I stand in politics that was natural and inevitable. But they handled him very stupidly and being the sort of man he was he reacted quite predictably.' Oliver looked away from her. 'We both know

44

what happened. I've heard it whispered that the British arranged his murder but I simply don't believe it. Whitehall doesn't own the simple guts to underwrite an assassination, but when the job had been done it suited them very nicely. So they got on with the plan they'd already made, which on the face of it wasn't a bad one. The constitution looked fine on paper, the nicest possible equilibrium between the Chinese and the rest of us. And in theory that still exists.' Oliver sighed unhappily, rubbing his chin. 'The trouble in practice is that we're not very good at running things. We like to take it easy and more materialistic people exploit us. When the Radens were there they pinched that out early—any arrogance by the Chinese, I mean—but now that we've got self-government I doubt if the paper balance will last. And so do most of my mother's race. They don't know what to do and it makes them frustrated—desperate. So they riot, like we saw.'

'We can't bring back the old days. They've gone for good.'

'I'm not a reactionary and I don't want to try.'

She frowned, considering. 'But there must be a Malay with political guts, a man who can keep his end up, his people's with it.'

'I thought once there wasn't but now I'm not sure.'

'What's his name?'

'I don't know his real one. I only met him once when his men came and rescued me.'

'You didn't tell me you had to be rescued.'

Those Chinese would have me still if I hadn't been.' He held up a gloved hand again. 'But I don't want to talk of that now or ever.'

'But you must tell me why you're in England.'

'I can't,' he said shortly.

Yet he looked at her, weighing her metal. She was an intelligent woman but also a very young one. He hadn't the right to commit her to *Realpolitik*.

Sheila for her part could sense the half-truth. Well, she wouldn't hurry him—she needn't. She asked, sounding casual:

'You've got friends here?'

'Several, and they're increasing.'

'Good friends?'

For a moment he dropped back into his careful old-fashioned English. 'They seem,' he said deliberately, 'to cover a very wide range of jobs.'

'Not just bods from the High Commissioner's?'

He laughed aloud. 'The High Commission is split from top to bottom. They're all waiting to see which way the ball will spin at home. Then they'll go with it if they haven't already chosen.'

'If you've friends you'll have news too. You'll know that the High Commissioner has started a case against me. He says I've got the state's crown jewels and it's an insult.' She flared in sudden anger again. 'We're not damned white rajahs, we never were.'

'Yes, I knew about the case.'

'Is that why they tortured you—something to do with the jewellery? I couldn't bear it if I were responsible.'

'No, it was not.'

'Then is that what you've come to England for?'

'I'm not interested in the jewellery, or only very marginally.' She knew he was telling a part of the truth, she knew that it wasn't the whole of it. Very well, she would have to wait.

He looked at his watch again, rising to leave. She tried to push him down and failed. He stood surprisingly strongly and laughed at her.

'Oliver, you're infuriating. I think you're doing it on purpose.'

He said simply: 'I am—I have to. I'm not my own master and you're a young woman.'

'Please don't be pompous.'

He chuckled as he took her hand. She said:

'But I must know where you're living.'

He hesitated but answered at last. 'I've a room in Earls Court in a boarding-house called the Ransome. Not that I use it much. I flit around.'

'You're telling me you're on the run? The peculiar friends you spoke about, the police . . .?'

'Not quite that. I haven't yet broken the law but I do keep queer company.'

'Oliver, you're killing me. I'll come down to this Ransome and see you're made comfortable.'

'You're never to do that,' he said. 'Never.'

'But I can ring you there?'

'Yes and no.' He tore the flap from an old envelope, scribbling on the back. 'That's my contact at the Ransome, one of the friends I spoke about. He's also the night porter. He might tell you where I am or he might not.'

'I could kick you and enjoy it.' Instead she kissed him warmly.

'Steady,' he said, 'I'm a big boy now.'

She kissed him again. 'And I'm your cousin. Call it a cousinly kiss.'

He gave her a look which froze her levity on her lips; he said in his careful English again: 'If that was a cousinly kiss I'd be interested in the other sort.' He picked up his hat and walked to the door. He didn't look back at her.

When he had gone she sat down with a third brew of tea. Sleep would be impossible, she didn't even consider it. Something was happening, something exciting. She had known him too well to delve too hard, trying to force his confidence and shutting him up at once. And the *Worldline* programme had shaken her, partly the grim violence and partly something else which she couldn't pin. She had an almost masculine hatred of loose ends and she started to chase her emotion. She decided it wasn't a difficult chase: once you faced it the fact was obvious. The emotion had been nostalgia. Sheila Raden was bitterly homesick.

She sighed for it wasn't convenient. She'd come back to England to make her life; she'd been trained as an almoner, a useful job she was doing well. Now it was meaningless, dust and ashes. . . . Or a well-heated house in Wimbledon and two or three well-behaved children? She knew she wouldn't stand it for the years she would need to bear them. It didn't have to be Geoffrey Addis but it would be somebody very like him, kind, amiable and a gentleman. She would have liked to live as her father had, able to visit England when he wanted to shoot or needed to shop. That alas would be impossible.

She realized now that so was any sort of England as her life. Houses in upper suburbia, pleasant clean husbands who smelt doggily of after-shave, the fruits of considerate love-making, not particularly clumsy and very possibly not quite ignorant, but . . .

But it was futile to deceive oneself, a white but alien, infidel woman.

She woke in her chair at eleven and rang her hospital. She hadn't meant to sleep nor thought she could.

In the comfortable house in Wimbledon Clement Addis was listening to Dorothy, his wife. They were talking in her bedroom and she hadn't invited him in for several years. She was weeping, near hysteria, but he wasn't paying attention to that. In a handful of simple sentences she had just destroyed his life.

He knew that she was a gambler since it was one of the ways she'd been bleeding him. There'd been others, he thought grimly now, absurdly expensive debts at absurdly expensive shops, a lover who in turn had been bleeding Dorothy. No more than a leak at first and then a flood, a streaming staunchless river of debt. He'd been more than remiss in not grasping the nettle, but he was old, she'd seemed to love him once, and when he'd told himself from time to time that he was excusing himself for cowardice, then behind the moment's realism stood an old man's distaste for a row, a scene. It simply wasn't dignified and at seventy a man must have that or a man would have nothing at all.

He was treating her now with a sort of exhausted courtesy. 'I knew that you gambled but not that big.'

'I swear to you I didn't mean——'

'It's done,' he said wearily. 'Let it lie.'

'We can't. I gave a cheque.'

'On your own account? It bounced?' He was talking as he might have talked to a foolish but favourite daughter. It might have been a tenner instead of a straight ten thousand pounds.

She nodded at him miserably.

'Let them whistle,' he said briefly, 'let them sue. The debt's legally irrecoverable.' There was a flash of a much younger man. 'Letting a woman play for that money . . . I'll have to resign from my club I expect, and it'll hardly be advertisement for the business which buys our bread.' He was tempted to add but characteristically did not: 'And up to recently some butter.' Instead he said firmly: 'They've had enough from me and mine.'

She stared at him in horror. 'You mean you won't pay?'

'I mean that I can't.'

'But you don't understand. I lost it at the Gardenia.'

He shrugged for it meant nothing.

'Don't you ever read the newspapers?'

With the first hint of anger he told her that he did. 'But not the ones in the gutter. I can live without gossip about fashionable gambling clubs.'

'I must make you understand, I *must*. The Gardenia's the Gardenia.'

'It sounds less fragrant than the flower,' he said. The tiny joke mildly pleased him.

It pushed Dorothy Addis from near-hysteria into a real one. She made a sound, half scream, half choke. 'They sent men here, they threatened me. They showed me a razor and a bottle of acid.'

She'd been sitting up in bed but now collapsed. Clement hardly heard her weeping. For a moment he sat as still as a rock, then he rose and walked out steadily. He walked steady as an ancient stone and suddenly was as ancient.

CHAPTER FOUR

Colonel Charles Russell had been doing his homework. He wouldn't have used the phrase himself since it smelt of Whitehall habits which he heartily despised, the man who had done his homework, the boy who knew all the answers, the busy Treasury bumblebee with his bland assumption that an official who'd mugged his papers up had done everything required of him, everything humanly possible.

It was an attitude which infuriated him but it didn't decrease his respect for the facts. One had to know them to get anywhere, and Russell had promised Harry Tuke that he'd do the little possible. He liked Harry Tuke and admired him too: his colloquial style was congenial, an agreeable change from the grim northern gratings or the calculated outbursts of a candour which told you nothing. Harry Tuke had once said it was touch and go in Shahbaddin. That was his way of talking, very possibly exaggerated if you held him to it literally. Charles Russell didn't intend to. Tuke might put it in three words and an official might have mistrusted them, but Russell hadn't a shadow of doubt that if Shahbaddin was worrying Tuke it should be worrying Charles Russell too.

And any other realist who happened to have a hand on the levers of power. There didn't seem, nowadays, to be many about.

Russell had undertaken to keep an eye on Oliver Raden, and this he had done discreetly. The results had been negative, as in a case of this sort he'd expected. There wasn't in fact a case at all, or not in the sense that colleagues down the road would have thought of cases. There wasn't even a useful clue, just a pile of fresh dossiers which his machine had thrown up to him.

He looked at them, reflecting, for he had read them more

than once . . . Oliver Raden, alias Kendry—almost nothing. He was what Charles Russell had thought he was, the illegitimate son of the Raden who would have inherited if he'd hadn't died prematurely. He had the tastes of a scholar, old books and his country's history, and he'd scrupulously avoided the least involvement in local politics. He could have visited England for a dozen innocent reasons or none at all. He'd been met at the airport by a Malay? But why not? And he'd been meeting other Malays who lived in London? Why not again? Nothing was known against any of his contacts, or rather nothing political, which was the Executive's limited interest, meticulously observed. As for the High Commissioner, the man who was bringing this troublesome lawsuit, every man in Whitehall with access to information knew all about His Excellency. His office was split in two racial factions, but equally so was his country. In any case High Commissioners hardly counted. It was a job for a politician who hadn't quite made it. He'd take orders from his government and watch which way the wind blew. Then he'd go with it, a consenting straw.

Russell put these two files on one side. The next was more interesting. Sheila Raden—ah! A young beauty of generous means which might soon be more, one who worked in a hospital and was reported to be good at it. Naturally she would be. Russell looked at the photograph: the chin was firm but in no way stubborn, the eyes were steady though not yet alight. It was an excellent likeness but he considered it short of justice, for he'd met Sheila Raden and remembered it with a pleasant glow. It had been at one of those parties to which Russell went in duty. Mostly they bored him cruelly but this one hadn't. Sheila Raden had made his evening, treating him quite beautifully. A huddle of much younger men had been hanging about in waiting, but Sheila had made it perfectly plain that she'd rather chat with an older man. An older man? Quite so, but still a man. She'd done it superbly, half, he'd suspected, just the instincts of gentle breeding, but the other half a woman's art, a mature and surprisingly expert skill. There'd been respect in her manner and a subtle sort of flattery, but also something else and she'd let him see it. He might be older than those others, but he was still a male animal. Yes, and very much so.

Charles Russell had purred appreciatively.

He put Sheila Raden's file away, turning to the fourth and last. He knew Addis too since he'd met him shooting. Russell shot competently or he wouldn't have shot at all, but he wasn't in Addis's class or near it. Clement Addis, he decided, must be one of the dozen best guns alive. It had been partridges in Norfolk, not the pheasants from a high belt of wood which Russell could take and mostly did, but partridges across a hedge, coming at forty which seemed like a hundred. Russell simply couldn't manage them; he'd miss twice in front, then maybe shoot a brace up the bottom. But Addis was taking two in front before Charles Russell had done his missing, then he'd change his gun smoothly and collect two more behind. The classic two in front and two behind. Like anything done perfectly it had undeniably been beautiful.

Russell had been incredulous when they'd told him that Addis was nearly seventy. He looked twenty years younger and shot like a man of forty. Russell hadn't quite believed them but now he did, for he'd seen Clement Addis the evening before. He'd been taken to Addis's club and there he'd seen him. He'd been drinking at the bar and rather a lot. And he'd looked his age and even more, an old man drinking heavily.

Charles Russell read the file again, frowning, a little uneasy. It was the sort of dossier he detested, setting his teeth on a warning edge. It was there, every detail, and when you came to it there was nothing. An old man with a much younger wife, not a wholly nasty woman but a stupid. There was a fine home in Wimbledon but a flat in London too. Charles Russell, a tolerant man, approved: there were worse ways of running that sort of *ménage*. But Dorothy Addis hadn't always been clever. It was one thing to have a man at call, quite another to give him money. It wasn't as though she were old, she was still attractive. And a flat in London cost money, too. Could Mastertons afford that now, could Clement, could anyone?

There was her gambling on top of it. Dorothy Addis was a compulsive gambler which meant that she wasn't a good one.

Charles Russell sighed for he hated messes, an old man betrayed, not so much in his bed which he'd be wise enough to overlook as his wife would be too sensible to throw the calendar in his face; but in his business, his links with life. Mastertons *was* something. It stood for a world which Charles Russell for one did not wish to see repeated, but if the waters were rolling over it they had left it its sheen, a certain air. That wasn't so common that it should be destroyed unthinkingly. Destroyed by a changing society perhaps, but not broken casually by the wife of its master. Family businesses were in any case struggling. To use Harry-Tuke-talk it was mostly touch and go with them.

There were very ugly rumours and they were growing.

Charles Russell's reflections were interrupted by his secretary. 'Chief Superintendent Willis,' she said. 'If you could spare him a moment——'

'Of course.'

She showed in the Chief Super and Russell asked him to sit down. He didn't offer him a drink because he didn't yet know him well enough. Of the various senior policemen with whom Russell had working relations he probably knew George Willis least, and for a very good reason which both understood. Chief Superintendent Willis dealt with ordinary, non-political crime. Theft, for instance, and misappropriation. He was a sharp-eyed man and he used them now.

'If it doesn't sound impertinent, sir, I couldn't help noticing that file you've got in front of you. The cover says "Clement Addis".'

'It does.'

'That might make this interview easier.'

'I hope you didn't think it was going to be difficult.'

'Not exactly difficult, simply tricky to open the subject. But now I can see you've an interest in Clement Addis it's more straightforward.'

'Not exactly in the man, but his firm holds a safe which has

53

awkward political overtones. But you'll have done your own guessing if you're interested in the case at all.'

'Do you mind if I put my hand down?' The Chief Superintendent smiled. 'It's usually wiser with the Security Executive.'

Russell said amiably: 'Meaning you'll lay four down and keep one up?'

Willis wasn't offended. 'All right sir, I'll lay down four.' He considered, then began to recite. 'First we naturally know that the High Commissioner is suing the Raden family for jewels which he says are the state's, not theirs. Secondly, since we read the newspapers, we know that things in Shahbaddin are pretty dicy.' The Chief Super looked bland. 'In those circumstances it wouldn't surprise the police if the Executive held a watching brief.'

'What makes you think that?'

'We're experienced guessers,' George Willis said.

'I'm not formally denying that I've an interest.'

'Thank you, sir, that helps us on.'

'So that was two cards. I suggest another.'

'I'll put down a couple again. The third is this court injunction. The Radens kept their jewellery in a safe at Mastertons, and there's an injunction that nothing should leave it till the court case has been decided.' For a second Willis hesitated. 'The fourth card I'd call that file on your desk.'

'Clement Addis?'

'Yes—personally.'

'You know he's privately embarrassed?'

'Pretty embarrassed. And some of the why.'

'Very well,' Russell said, 'so you've got one up your sleeve still.'

'Not exactly a card, sir. A thing. An article.' Willis had a dispatch case and he opened it now deliberately. He put on the table a woman's tiara of diamonds.

'And what in the world is that?'

'I'm not an expert in these matters at all. If it had strawberry leaves or whatnot I'd have called it a coronet.'

'I don't think it's that, not technically.' Russell looked at it carefully. 'Is it genuine?' he inquired.

'Entirely. Fifty thousand quid's worth or thereabouts. It didn't cost that much when whoever first bought it did so, but that's today's value.'

'May I ask where you got it?'

'I got it from a fence. He wouldn't relish the word since he's a member of a club—all that—and he's also running a straight business as his cover. So he doesn't take risks, not unreasonable risks. He thought he'd seen this toy before so he brought it straight to me. He gave ten thousand pounds for it, so he's ten thousand out by coming to the police, but that's chicken feed to my good friend the fence, much better than losing his business and doing time.'

'You have pretty odd friends.'

'And haven't we all?'

Charles Russell let that one pass. It was fair enough comment and he wanted to think. He asked at last:

'Why did the fence come to you?'

'Because he thought he knew the owners. His legitimate business is also a jeweller's, though it's rather different from Mastertons. He's in a pretty close trade and his memory is excellent. He thought he'd seen this thing before and a Raden head had been wearing it.'

'So that's a Raden tiara?'

'On any reasonable bet it is.'

'Which means it must have come from the safe at Mastertons.'

'Which means, I'm afraid, it could have.'

Charles Russell was silent, fingering the Addis file. This was the end of the road for Clement Addis.

'What are you going to do?' he asked.

'That's why I came to see you, sir—we might just possibly oblige each other. There are two possible courses open and only two.' Willis was in the saddle now, not pressingly but aware of it. 'There's a young woman called Sheila Raden and *prima facie* she's the owner. If this is really her family property then she'll certainly have seen it. We could fetch her up and ask her.'

'And if she confirms it's hers?'

'Bang goes old Clement Addis on your desk.'

'And would you object to that?'

'I can't afford to object to things, I'm only a senior police-man. Contacting Sheila Raden is the easy way to handle it. The orthodox way too. The reason I'm here lies in the first four cards I put down for you. There are political complications in this or I wouldn't have come at all.'

'You're a very good friend,' Charles Russell said.

'That's really very handsome, sir, but you'll see that we've still got to know. Political complications or not, we can't shut our eyes to common crime.'

'I wouldn't have suggested it.'

'I know. Which brings me to the second course, but we're not anxious to embark on it unless the Executive finds it helpful. I used the plural and meant it for I've spoken to my superiors.'

'Fair enough—more than fair.'

George Willis said deliberately: 'Sheila Raden lives in Chelsea, in a duplex in a block of them. She's an almoner in a hospital and she goes there by tube every day. She walks to Sloane Square station, wet or fine. She isn't a buff for exercise but she like to keep her bowels open. She looks like it too. The girl's got a figure——'

'You seem to have checked up on her.'

'Of course. So she walks to Sloane Square and there's a jeweller on a corner.'

Russell said: 'Don't tell me. He's another of your friends.'

'He once did time but that's all forgotten. Or not quite forgotten in the sense that he'll still oblige me.'

'So your friend would co-operate?'

'He would.' Willis nodded at the tiara. 'By putting that thing in his window where Miss Raden is bound to see it. No woman under seventy passes a jeweller in her stride.'

'Excellent observation. And then?'

'Then if it isn't hers she'll do nothing at all. But if she recognizes it she'll go to the police.'

'Which would still put Clement Addis in jail.'

'That's inevitable if my fence was right, but we shouldn't have a dead-straight line to that awkward safe you spoke about —that awkward safe politically. Not on a mere sighting in a Chelsea jeweller's window. There'd be every sort of inquiry to make and we'd have to walk pretty carefully. And that would take time, perhaps quite a lot of it.' Willis looked at Charles Russell levelly. 'It was our impression you could use a little elbow-room. I mean on the political side. *Your* side.'

'I'm really very grateful and one day I'll do the same for you.'

'That, sir,' said Willis coolly, 'was my superiors' idea.'

Sheila Raden was returning with Geoffrey Addis from a party to which he'd taken her. She hadn't much wished to go but Geoffrey had pressed her. The hosts, it seemed, were important people and customers of Mastertons too; the party, he'd assured her, would be quite first-rate. She'd accepted at last since she didn't want to offend him, conscious moreover of another reason for his insistence. Behind the important people and the promised distinguished party lay a motive rather more human and to Sheila much more creditable. Geoffrey Addis liked to be seen with her—she was a flower in his buttonhole of the nicest possible kind. She'd said yes at last, but without enthusiasm. That sort of party wasn't her meat.

And now as the taxi ground them home she was wishing she hadn't gone. For the evening had ended in near-disaster. It hadn't been Geoffrey's fault, she thought; she was a fair-minded girl and she couldn't blame him. But he might have been more effective in the pinch.

She'd been sitting drinking orangeade and Geoffrey had left her for more champagne. Into the empty chair slipped Miss Moira Perry. And Sheila hadn't been warned about Moira Perry. She was an iron-grey woman of fifty-plus, a distinguished civil servant who'd have been even more distinguished if men hadn't hated working with her. She'd carefully scissored her chin for the party, and she'd been waiting her chance at Sheila, sweating like a stallion. Those who knew her had seen the symptoms and had been variously amused by them, but nobody had thought worth while to pass the tip to Sheila. Moira Perry weighed knocking thirteen stone and she decanted them deliberately into Geoffrey's vacant chair. She began to make small-talk in a well-modulated baritone.

Sheila didn't rumble her, or not till the occasion was out of control. She'd written Moira off as a gabby old bag of fifty-odd, one with a funny voice who had let herself go. She'd read books about unorthodox tastes but had never met them. Moira Perry didn't click with her, or not at first.

Quite soon the coin dropped embarrassingly clearly. Sheila pushed Moira's hand from her stockinged thigh, for the moment more astonished than offended. She looked at Moira uneasily. She was shivering now and the room wasn't cold; her lips were drawn back over yellowing teeth, her rather fine eyes were glazing. She was more than a little in splendid wine and dizzy with lust to edge the drink.

The hand came up again, bolder and much higher now, and Sheila again removed it. This woman was clearly lethal. . . . Throw her drink in Moira's face? Unseemly. Then simply get up and walk away? It was the sort of thing which attracted attention, and it was Sheila's impression, wrongly, that they hadn't been too much noticed. She looked around the room for help. Geoffrey still had his back to her, but three young men were hovering near.

She upset her orangeade.

The posse of hopefuls had been waiting for their moment, descending on Sheila compactly. One bore champagne which was poor observation. She thanked him with a smile but shook her head. The second had Cola which made her sick. She ignored the man with Cola, but the third had orangeade.

'How kind of you, and how very, er, quick. Won't you sit down and talk to me?'

Moira Perry sighed but she knew when she'd had it. She heaved herself upright, turning a basilisk stare on the three young men. Then she waddled away, old and a little horrible, ridiculous but pitiable too.

Now, in the taxi, Sheila was shaken. She'd known there were woman of Moira's kind as she'd known there were pygmies in Africa; she hadn't expected to meet one and the encounter had outraged her. Geoffrey shouldn't have taken her, or if that was unfair and he hadn't known, then at least he should keep his eyes skinned, watch his women. They were almost at her flat and she looked from the taxi's window. On an impulse she said: 'I'd like to walk.' The cool evening air would clear her head and when she got home she'd wash from scalp to toe. Not in a bath, though in England she mostly used them, but in fresh running water, the proper way.

Geoffrey offered his arm but Sheila didn't seem to notice it. They turned right from the King's Road, then left. On the corner was a jeweller, the light in the window burning still, and Sheila glanced in indifferently. She'd passed it several hundred times and could have inventoried the contents. This time she stopped in her tracks and stared. She stared again.

No, there couldn't be the slightest doubt.

She looked sideways at Geoffrey Addis. He was looking in the window too but his English face told her nothing at all.

. . . Well, he could hardly comment. But if he'd seen it and kept quiet it meant . . .

They walked on to her duplex and at the foot of the stairs he said it. 'I'm sorry about that woman. I was told about it afterwards.'

'It wasn't you fault. Don't worry.'

He didn't attempt to kiss her and she let him go composedly. She went up to her room and opened her bag, and when she had found the paper she dialled the number.

'Is that the Ransome hotel?'

'It is.' The voice wasn't English.

'I want to speak to the night porter.'

'Speaking.'

She switched suddenly to Malay. 'I was given your name by a mutual friend.'

A pause. 'That's possible.'

'Can you contact our friend?'

'I think so.'

'Then please do. I must see him urgently.' She gave her address and the name of Sheila Raden.

'Did you say Raden?'

'Yes.'

'Expect a visit in half an hour, it'll take me that to reach him.'

She settled to wait, her mind in a whirl, trying not to think about Geoffrey Addis.

Who had run to the nearest call-box, telephoning the house in Wimbledon. Dorothy's voice had answered him.

'Is that Dorothy? How are you? I'd like to speak to father, please.'

He didn't approve of Dorothy Addis but studiously kept good relations. Nevertheless he spoke of his father, never, to her, of Clement.

'I'm afraid he isn't very well.'

'Nothing serious, I hope.'

'It depends on how you look at it.'

He considered it quickly since this wasn't Dorothy Addis's form. He thought her a tiresome woman, a disaster for his father, but she wasn't an evasive one. On the contrary she'd normally blurt things out.

'Has he been drinking?'

'Yes he has.'

Geoffrey sighed softly. He knew that his father had been hitting the bottle, but many old men took that drink or two too many and so far Clement's drinking, though admittedly rather heavy, had been notably short of scandalous. He said to gain time:

'Then I hope he's all right.'

'I hope so too, but he's out like a light.'

From anybody but Dorothy Geoffrey wouldn't have

believed it. Clement Addis was now a drinking man but he'd never passed out in his life. 'He's in bed, of course?'

'Of course.'

'Will he be making the office tomorrow?'

'Your guess is as good as mine.'

'Take care of him.'

'But naturally,' she said coldly.

Geoffrey Addis hung up and went back to his flat. His face was taut, he looked suddenly middle-aged. So he might be seeing his father next day or again he might not be meeting him. It wasn't perhaps important now since tomorrow would be too late.

Oliver Raden had arrived at Sheila's duplex. The thirty minutes predicted had been an underestimate by twenty, and Sheila had waited impatiently. But now he was present he was reassuringly collected; he listened to her excited tale; he considered it and then summed up.

'You're certain that tiara you saw was really your mother's?'

'Positive. I've often seen her wear it.'

'It might have been a replica.' He sounded a little doubtful still.

'I know nothing about the jewellery trade but I don't think they make replicas of that sort of private order.'

He nodded, accepting it, retreating again into silent thought. Sheila looked at him in a quick contentment, conscious of a male presence. This gentle man with his wry smile and scholar's stoop could be deceptive. Now he looked concentrated, formidable, even dangerous. It was something she'd felt a need of, something to recognize gladly and accept. Sheila Raden was suddenly happy.

He said almost to himself: 'We've got to know very soon what's in that safe.' He added with a quick emphasis: '*Or even isn't.*'

'I'm not with you. Am I meant to be?'

The direct question he ducked. 'I don't credit the rubbish about crown jewels much more than you do. But there are rumours in Shahbaddin. . . .' He caught her eye and held it, for the second time weighing her metal. 'Aren't you interested in why I'm desperate to know what's in that safe?'

'No,' she said, 'not a bit.'

He was astonished and said so. 'But surely——'

She stopped him almost impatiently. 'It's really very simple. Whatever's still in that safe is either mine or it isn't, so either some judge will give it me, or if we lose the case he won't.'

'You've a frightening logical mind. But it's me now, not the judge, who wants to know what the safe contains. Or, as I ought to hint again, does not. Aren't you really interested in why?

'All right then, I'm curious. But I'm still not asking.' There was a silence which Sheila finally broke. 'When you were here last you talked about Shahbaddin. We watched a programme on the telly and I've been reading the newspapers since. There's a lot that you're not telling me, why they tortured you for instance, since it wasn't for the jewels. Even why you're in England at all.'

'I can't tell you. I daren't.'

She dismissed it imperiously. 'You'll tell me when you can, I've accepted that. Meanwhile I'm on Oliver Raden's side. *Our* side.'

'Are you telling me you'd help?' he asked.

'Don't you understand simple statements?'

'Do you mind if I smoke?'

'Stop treating me like a lady, please. I'm not feeling very ladylike.'

He lit another Dutch cheroot, blowing the smoke away from her. She had put him on a spot she didn't know. She alone, he was thinking, could perhaps pull it off, the plan which his friends had been too realistic to press strongly. But it would be compromising her and probably worse. The law was not mocked or at least not in England. Against that she knew Geoffrey Addis; she had the essential *entrée* to Mastertons. None of the others had that or anything like it. But Geoffrey Addis had been courting her—his friends had mentioned that too. One couldn't ask a woman to sell a future fiancé down the tide. He looked at Sheila shrewdly, hooding the glance. No, she wasn't in love with Geoffrey, that was sure. She wasn't in love with anyone yet but when, if at all, it hit her . . .

He collected his thoughts again. 'I haven't the right to ask for help.'

'Nor the right to prevent my offering it.'

'You don't know what you're risking,' he said.

'Not till you tell me—no.'

He struggled with his conscience, lost, making the frayed excuses of any man who was using a woman: she was mature enough to know her mind, the cause came first, the people second. He grimaced in distaste for he could recognize self-deception. But one thing he owed her as he'd owe anyone else who offered help. He'd tell her the risks and fairly, but he didn't now doubt she'd accept them.

'I've a possible idea,' he said. 'Maybe it's crazy.'

'Tell me.'

He told her.

He'd been afraid she might be scandalized or even worse laugh at him, but she took it with cool composure. 'You told me you had peculiar friends.'

He could laugh now himself. 'The man at the Ransome is only a porter but he's got plenty of other contacts. We're quite a flourishing organization if the word doesn't sound pretentious. There are some very stout hearts among my friends, and one in particular I like very much. He's a criminal by trade and doing well.'

'And he's the one you want me to help?'

'Don't put it like that.'

'Then he's the one I'm helping.'

'My God,' he said, 'you're a very cool hand.'

'Not a compliment to a woman but I know what you mean. I hope.'

'Then do you know the make of the safe?'

She shook her head.

'Or how long you've had it?'

'I know it can't be new. Father sometimes talked of changing it. It must be twenty years old or even thirty.'

'That ought to be enough for my talented friend.'

'Tell me,' she said, 'is this dangerous besides crazy?'

'Yes. Unless they believe you were simply a stooge and I don't think I would myself——'

'I didn't mean to me.'

'But I did. Unless they accept that you were simply being used by someone else they could put you in prison for quite a time.'

What she answered turned his heart over. 'Would I be old when they let me out?'

'No.' She could see he was telling the truth: when he could he always did. 'Three or four years at most, maybe less if you've got good lawyers.'

'I've got that all right, a Jew called Marks.'

'Then you can safely deduct a year at least.'

She lit a cigarette though she didn't smoke often. 'And supposing Geoffrey Addis doesn't buy it?'

He looked at her with a smile which was almost sly. 'It's my impression,' he said in English, 'that Mr Addis would do most things for your favour.'

'I know—that makes it worse.' She spoke with regret but with total decision. 'Just the same, I must know. If Geoffrey won't take the briefcase I can't put it under my bed.'

'No, I wouldn't advise it.' There was the rasp of the scholar's irony.

'Then what do I do?'

'You bring it back to me here at once. Here and immediately. Within an hour and a half of my delivering it to you myself. If that should be impossible you must throw it in the river.' He leant forward, adding sharply: 'Is that clear?'

'Perfectly clear. And when do I get your useful friend's briefcase?'

'I'll bring it round here at four tomorrow. That will give you till half-past five. Not a minute more.'

CHAPTER FIVE

Clement Addis hadn't expected to go to Mastertons next day, but after lunch he'd felt better and the disciplines of a lifetime were hard to break. Now he sat in his dignified office, numb. There was a note on his desk that his son had been trying to contact him but he pushed it aside indifferently. He wasn't feeling like Geoffrey or indeed like anyone else.

He wasn't, he realized, feeling at all, or not the emotions he'd once have expected. . . . Misappropriating a customer's property, a friend at that, and he a trustee of the dead friend's heir and daughter. These were terrible words but they'd somehow lost their bite for him. Uppermost in his mind was a sense of plain astonishment, not so much at the dreadful deed as that events should have forced him helplessly down a path which he found incredible. For never in his long lifetime had he been strapped for ten thousand pounds; he'd never even considered that he wouldn't be able to raise it.

But he hadn't, or not quickly enough, and it had shaken and humiliated him. He had an overdraft at his bank which he hadn't considered serious, though it would prevent him from taking a gun this year at Averley or anywhere else. But he'd used the same branch for forty years and the manager was his personal friend. If he'd slapped Clement's face he could hardly have surprised him more. There was a credit squeeze, he'd said, and other blah; he'd been desolated but . . .

The valuable house in Wimbledon then? Clement knew there was a mortgage but he'd almost forgotten the second. Subconsciously he'd wished to forget, to suppress the gnawing knowledge of how far his debts had swollen. His debts or Dorothy's: it didn't matter since he'd married her.

Typically he didn't blame her. She hadn't perhaps been an ideal wife for a man who was suddenly ageing, but he knew others of his contemporaries who had married younger women and fared much worse. The responsibility was his alone and he wasn't the man to decline it.

And there *was* a responsibility—he'd never doubted that from the moment she'd told him. Men from the Gardenia had threatened his wife—pay or take a faceful—and Clement Addis read the newspapers though not the same papers as Dorothy. Moreover he'd made an inquiry about the place they called the Gardenia. It might not happen, it probably wouldn't, but that sort of thing *had* happened. It was probably bluff but conceivably wasn't, and it wasn't the sort of bluff he could dare to call. The simple thought of Dorothy disfigured made Clement sick.

Or go to the police? And tell them how much? In any case, what could they guarantee? He couldn't keep a healthy woman mewed up in a house for ever.

Then the almost frantic search for ready cash. He could have raised money on the business but not quickly. There would be documents and assignments, a great pother with the lawyers. That meant time and he couldn't afford it. The business mightn't be what once it had been, but at least it was still unencumbered. Unencumbered but not ready cash, and he had deadly need of ten thousand pounds.

He'd been desperate when he'd met Jim Sender, whom he didn't much care for but inevitably knew. For Jim was another jeweller. His business was bigger though it hadn't Mastertons' cachet, and a year or so ago he'd been elected to Clement's club. Clement had been surprised but he'd realized the world was changing; he'd been surprised because Sender was tough and brash and also he'd heard the rumours. A generous man, he hadn't believed them but he could credit the possibility. What conceivably better front for a high-class fence than a prosperous jewellers as cover?

He'd gone down to his club for lunch, entirely miserable, and Sender had offered a drink at the bar. Clement had accepted since it was impossible to refuse, and in any case he needed a drink. Sender had started talking and Clement had almost dropped his drink. For Sender was propositioning him, crudely but it was business. Jim would like a piece of Mastertons and he had ready cash to back his fancy.

At any other moment Clement Addis would have been crusty, saying something stuffy about a club where one didn't talk business, but he couldn't afford idiosyncrasies now, he needed hard cash and he needed it fast. But he hadn't yet lost his business sense. He said non-committally:

'I don't say it's quite impossible but of course we'd have to talk seriously. Then there'd have to be lawyers and all the formalities.'

'Don't I know it—I loathe lawyers.' Jim Sender had looked at Clement hard. 'So frankly I'd like a string meanwhile.'

'A string?'

'That's right. An earnest that we're serious.' He finished his drink and Addis bought him another. 'I'll give you ten thousand pounds,' Jim said.

'For what?'

'Legally speaking for nothing. Between ourselves as an unofficial option that you don't do a deal elsewhere.'

'Why should I? If you think——'

'No offence,' Sender said. He was far too shrewd to press an apology; he shrugged but produced a cheque book; he wrote a cheque for ten thousand pounds and handed it to Clement. 'It's unofficial, of course—that's understood. So you can send me a piece to balance it. Any piece. I'll give you a receipt for that but the cheque doesn't need one.'

Clement fingered the cheque. If this was the modern manner it wasn't for him. He opened his mouth but shut it again. Ten thousand pounds. He heard himself say: 'As you wish.'

He took a taxi to his bank and paid in the cheque; he wrote another and posted it; he then went home to Dorothy. He felt reprieved, almost young again.

It wasn't till the evening that he began to assess his commitment to Sender. It was a harder one than he'd thought when he'd clutched the straw. He must send him a piece as collateral and he had several pieces worth ten thousand pounds. But they were very much part of the stock-in-trade: he couldn't remove one without somebody knowing and the first somebody would be Geoffrey. In his way he was a model son but he wasn't a man to share a father's troubles gracefully. Besides, if it came to taking a piece out Clement could just as well have sold it, though if he did that he'd be taking a loss, the swingeing loss which in any forced sale was inevitable. And he couldn't afford a swingeing loss.

It came up on him insidiously, unwelcome as the gout he sometimes carried. He knew the combination of the Raden family safe, as Geoffrey Addis knew it too, but Geoffrey wouldn't be using it, not with this injunction on. And it would have to be the tiara since there wasn't another piece of equal value. It was worth several times ten thousand pounds but Sender wouldn't object to that. He'd accept the extra value as an earnest of good intentions, perhaps even as a compliment to the standing of his own business. It hadn't seemed like stealing at the time.

Clement had managed to live with it for a day and a little over when the black thought had struck him down. He'd done business with Jim Sender in a moment of desperation, intending to fix the final deal fast, when he'd naturally get the tiara back before the case, now postponed, came on. Of course it wasn't honest, it went flatly against a lifetime's standards, but perhaps it could be called pardonable, the mere borrowing of a collateral until the genuine asset of a share in his firm could be negotiated at a proper price. Just like a loan from the bank if not so orthodox.

Except for one thing, though it was only a rumour. If Sender really had a second trade Clement Addis would be finished. He'd have passed stolen goods to a professional fence, and if the fence should happen to realize it he'd have the hooks in Clement Addis. Whichever way you looked at it that wouldn't be very healthy. Blackmail, Clement Addis thought, or a sell-out to the police. . . .

He was sitting thinking grimly when his secretary interrupted him. 'Mr Geoffrey would like to see you, please.'

'Tell him,' he said unhappily, 'that I'm much too tired to talk to him.'

Upstairs at Mastertons Clement Addis was brooding miserably and downstairs, in a smaller room, Geoffrey was talking to Sheila Raden. The time was twenty minutes to five.

He'd been surprised at her voice on the telephone since she'd never rung him at the business, but he'd agreed at once to see her. It had been her second important call of the day, the first had been to David Marks. He'd been curious at her inquiry, cautious like the good lawyer he was, but he hadn't asked outright why she put the question. Instead he'd read the injunction over, repeating a passage twice at her request. Then he'd invited her to dinner and with a certain regret she had turned him down. David Marks had his defects but undeniably he was stimulating.

Now she was sitting opposite Geoffrey Addis. His office doubled as interview room, a place where he could receive such customers as were too important to trade across a counter or more likely simply believed they were. The room was small but held some fine Georgian furniture, and from her comfortable chair Sheila looked hard at Geoffrey. She had realized now that she would never have married him. She had an acquaintance of progressive views, and this lady's tiresome cliché for a marriage to Geoffrey Addis would have been legalized prostitution. Sheila Raden didn't think like that. A woman wanted security and must expect to pay the normal price. Most did and it wasn't intolerable. Not legalized prostitution then—married women never talked like that unless they'd messed up their marriage already—but inescapably legalized something and with Geoffrey it wouldn't be legalized sex. It would be very much harder to live with than that, a lifetime of total propriety. Besides, there was something behind the careful façade, some streak she could sense but couldn't pin. Behind the gentlemanly front could be another Geoffrey Addis, and an increasing instinct warned her that it might very well be the real one. It mattered not in the least to her, since she had written off Geoffrey and England too.

She held up the briefcase, saying matter-of-factly: 'I want you to put that in our safe.'

'But you know I can't do that.'

Sheila suppressed a shrug. It was the conditioned response she'd been warned to expect and she'd prepared herself to answer. Just the same it was a nuisance, this tedious spelling it out.

'I don't see why not.'

'But the injunction,' he said. It was on the tip of his tongue to tell her that this was the second time he'd been asked to ignore the law, but Kin had tried to bribe him and that wasn't the sort of story you passed to a young woman. It wasn't a story you passed on at all unless you could prove it beyond shadow of doubt, and Geoffrey well knew that he couldn't do that. Moreover Sheila wasn't bribing him, she wasn't like Kin in any way, but was talking a kind of inverted sense. She'd begun to explain in a neutral voice, trying to sound convincing and at the same time not to offend him. Men hated it when a woman knew better.

'I know about the injunction and I know what it says exactly. It's an undertaking that nothing should be removed from that safe till some judge says you can. It says nothing at all about putting things in.'

He looked at her sharply. 'They sent you a copy?'

'No, but my lawyer has one.'

'And you've been checking on the terms with him?'

'Naturally, or I wouldn't be here.'

She saw that she'd make a solid point, that he was solidly considering it. She was disliking herself but not too much. She wasn't going to marry him, she owed him nothing by emotion. Nevertheless she wished him no harm and she was putting him on a serious risk. Well, she was risking much more herself. Oliver had told her that they could jail her for three or four years. This time she didn't suppress her shrug. Her conscience was clear or at least anaesthetized. It wasn't a Christian organ, but practical and elastic. More important it was a female.

Geoffrey said doubtfully: 'But why do you want me to put this in the safe?'

She'd expected the question, rehearsed the answer. Since there wasn't a good one she was going to give none. 'The Radens have been dealing here for a good many generations.'

She hadn't meant it as an open threat but as the sort of slick appeal which privately made her shudder. Geoffrey made it a little easier when he took it as simple blackmail. He stiffened at once and his blue eyes narrowed. For a moment she thought he looked almost a man, almost like Oliver when he was angry or thinking intently. But his words let his look down fatally.

'Really,' he said, 'I'd hardly expected—'

'I had reason to hope you'd help, that's all.'

'Yet you won't tell me why.'

She shook her head.

'And I'd been wondering about us, even hoping . . .'

He realized at once that he'd made a mistake: instead of his softening her she'd hardened. Besides, she was thinking, he was giving her that stare again. It held an evident calculation which for the first time now was overt, but also a real desire. But not her kind. It was the desire of an English gentleman in very high-class retail trade.

She simply didn't want him.

Geoffrey fingered the bag, then picked it up. He seemed surprised by its weight but he didn't comment. 'Very well,' he said finally, 'I'll do as you wish.' He put on the 'you' a faint but significant emphasis. Sheila caught it but wasn't moved.

'Thank you,' she said, 'you're very kind.'

He gave her a sideways smile she hadn't yet seen; he might have been sharing a joke with her but he hadn't that sort of humour. In fact almost none. That was one of her private excuses for conduct she knew was hard to excuse. But the smile had been there, crooked and even cynical. It made him more interesting but not quite enough. As he walked her to the door he asked:

'Can I get you a taxi?'

'Don't trouble, the doorman will find one. And thanks again.'

In the taxi she looked at her watch. It was ten past five and fifteen minutes to her flat. The half hour with Geoffrey had seemed much longer.

Back in the duplex Oliver Raden rose to meet her. He was tense as an exploding spring and asked her before she had shut the door: 'Did it go all right?'

'He took it—yes.'

He looked at the clock. 'You cut it pretty fine,' he said.

'You were worried?'

'Like hell.'

. . . He looked worried all right. For their plan, for the safety of an accomplice, for Sheila Raden . . .?

He crossed the room and took her hand. 'Good girl,' he said. 'Good girl.' It was a banality but it shattered her. He lifted her hand to his mouth but she took it away. He looked at her, then spread his arms.

It was the gesture she had been waiting for.

Mastertons stayed open till six o'clock, but the late evening trade was by no means the most important and Geoffrey normally left at half-past five. He was standing on the front doorstep, lighting a cigarette, wishing the uniformed doorman a courteous goodnight. He thought it wise to keep in with servants. The door was open behind them but there wasn't a draught. Nevertheless Geoffrey's lighter went out. The air came by him solidly, not so much a blast as a compact and sensible shock wave. The fine plate glass window fell deliberately into the street, its noise as it broke on the pavement a single crack. The splendid Royal Warrant teetered, then fell too. Perhaps significantly it fell upright and on its feet. An alarm bell clanged noisily.

And someone had blown them. Mastertons.

Geoffrey ran through the showroom, down the stairs to the basement. At its entrance was a formidable grille. He killed the alarm system, unlocking the grille with the key he always carried. There was an ante-chamber first, leading to the real strongroom, the steel door of the latter shining dully in the opposite wall, a single electric light bulb picking an occasional highlight from the chromium dials controlling its combination. Geoffrey frowned. So he'd left the electric light on when he'd been here twenty minutes ago. That had been careless but now was unimportant.

It had always astonished him that people of means should keep valuables in safes which a competent amateur could break in minutes. There were at least half a dozen of them, conveniences to established customers. Mastertons charged a modest rent but insisted it wasn't a safe deposit. Still, the security was considerable, an up-to-date alarm system and the formidable grille which Geoffrey had just unlocked again, but it was neither better nor worse than Mastertons thought necessary for the lesser of their stock-in-trade which they kept outside the strongroom proper. They always emphasized that, made the customer sign a paper before they'd even consider giving houseroom to that customer's own safe.

And what antiquated things they mostly were. Incredible! Geoffrey ran to the Raden safe and stared. He'd seen safes blown before but never from inside out. He nodded appreciatively—it was a very neat job indeed. It would have been easy to blow the shop sky high, but it was a characteristic of good safecrackers as it was of competent surgeons too that they liked to use the minimum force. The door sagged on one old-fashioned hinge, there was the faintest smell of expended gelly. And that was all.

Almost literally, for the safe had been nearly empty. There were a handful of rings and trinkets, scattered, and a pearl necklace which Geoffrey knew was cultured. The settings might be twisted, but any stone which was genuine needn't be seriously damaged. There also some charring leather, smoking greyly, and Geoffrey winced. He wouldn't touch the pieces yet, not till the police had finished their business. They'd be here at any minute now since the alarm was wired to the local station. He wouldn't touch the pieces but he knew where they had come from. That briefcase Sheila had given him and . . .

A wave of humiliation shook him but a second thought doused his anger cold. Something was not in the safe and he knew it should be. The outer grille had still been locked so nobody could have got in to steal, far less escaped with the proceeds of theft. The police would delve for the motive later, but for the moment this wasn't a routine blow. But someone had blown it and there it was. Or rather was not. The only good thing, the Raden tiara.

Geoffrey was conscious that his father was standing beside him. He had a hand on the doorman's arm and was very white. He was staring into the safe, a man of seventy who looked ninety.

Geoffrey said: 'Father——' but Clement didn't answer him. He turned from the doorman and almost fell, then said dully to Geoffrey: 'See to it. Wait here for the police and see to it. I'm going upstairs.' He started to walk away and again almost fell. The doorman tried to steady him but he shook him off impatiently. He began to tackle the stairs with an effort which racked the watchers as it drained the last drops of an old man's courage. He walked rigidly, like a puppet, a broken man. But he walked alone.

Back in his room he sat down quietly. There was a single escape and he knew he could take it. Only one aspect worried him—the means. A shotgun would make an unseemly mess but he'd never owned a pistol in his life.

CHAPTER SIX

Charles Russell was in the Executive next morning, awaiting a visit from Chief Superintendent Willis. Willis had
asked for an interview urgently and Russell, who graded the
Chief Super high, had conceded it as promptly. Meanwhile
George Willis had sent him a paper. He was a busy man,
considerate of the time of others; he talked very well but was
impatient of explanations. A piece of paper did that better and
he had sent one round by hand. Charles Russell began to read it.

*Reference our previous conversation, the Raden safe at Mastertons
was blown at about five-thirty yesterday evening. So far the
newspapers know only that there was a blowing and that the
safe was under injunction, but there were in fact several unusual
features which I should like to discuss with you. I have my
superiors' authority to do so.*

Charles Russell nodded briefly. He'd seen a paragraph in
a late evening paper the night before. They'd had the name of
the man who had owned the safe and the name had been Sir
Montagu Raden. Russell had been interested but the story had
been very thin. He turned again to Willis's paper. This could
be the real one.

*The blowing was effected by means of an explosive charge.
This charge was contained in a leather briefcase which Mr Addis
junior deposited in the safe a few minutes before the actual
explosion. It was brought to him by a visitor whose name is
known. This is one of the aspects on which we should be grateful
for advice.*

Charles Russell sat up, his appetite whetted.

The Inspector first on the scene made a list of the safe's contents. There was less than you might imagine, our estimate being between fifteen hundred pounds' worth and two thousand.

. . . Awkward for Willis and me.

Mr Clement Addis had left the establishment but his son behaved with great correctitude. He produced the firm's own list of the safe's contents. That list included a diamond tiara, so the absence of the tiara is now known. That is the second aspect which my superiors wish me to discuss with you.

. . . I'll bet they do!

Finally, at nine o'clock this morning the cleaning-woman let herself into the Addis flat in Charlbert Street, N.W.8. Mr Clement Addis was alone and dead. He had blown most of his head off with the choke of a Purdey shotgun.

. . . Poor devil, poor fine old man.

Russell ordered coffee, and as Willis came in he gave him some. Willis looked at the desk and nodded. 'I see you've read my paper so we needn't waste time on the background. Where would you like me to start?'

'The tiara, I think, since we were both of us in the fiddle.'

The Chief Superintendent grimaced. 'I'm not popular with the big boys, sir.'

'They shouldn't be kicking your bottom if they authorized what we did themselves. I gathered from you they did.'

George Willis shrugged with a cheerful cynicism. 'You know the great. Not that that side's gone out of control—with luck. You can bend the law a bit—you and I bent it—but you can't play ducks and drakes with a Chancery judge.' His voice changed into a parody of a policeman's at Quarter Sessions. 'So acting on information received the police made inquiries about an allegedly missing property.' His voice came back to normal. 'It's conceded we're pretty fair at that and we found it rather promptly in a jewellers in Chelsea.'

'And where does that get you? I should have thought——'

'If everyone keeps their heads it lets both of us out. The jeweller, as I told you, is one of my peculiar friends. The tiara is worth around fifty thou, much too much for my good friend's business, but there's plenty of money in Chelsea still so he was showing it on commission for a very much bigger man called Sender. Who happens to be my other friend, the jeweller-fence who got it from Addis.'

'So far so good. But what story does the fence tell? Supposing, that is, he has to tell one.'

'The truth since he's obliged to—he gave a cheque. He gave Addis ten thousand as some sort of earnest-money on a proposition to buy into Mastertons and he asked for a piece as collateral. When the tiara came in he will say that it knocked him flat; he can tell a fifty-thousand bauble when he sees it. But he thought it over and then saw light, or so he'll swear if it's ever necessary. He decided that old Addis wasn't serious about selling a part of Mastertons, but it was known in the trade that he was desperately short of the ready. So this was in effect a very discreet forced sale. Old Addis would keep the money and Sender could keep the tiara and his mouth shut about where he got it. Addis was paying dearly for concealing that he was strapped, but it's astonishing the price men pay when they're wickedly pressed and as proud as Addis.'

Charles Russell considered it, finally nodding. 'So you protect your friends and sources as all good policemen ought to, and the small irregularity which you and I indulged in needn't come out at all.'

'But I'd like you to keep your fingers crossed.'

'And the tiara itself?'

'Not too embarrassing once we had a story for its recovery. We've told our official solicitor and he's gone into his legal trance. . . . What about the injunction? When was the tiara taken, before or after? Are we sure, can we swear to it? And ought we to tell that wretched High Commissioner too? There are apparently pros and cons which are beyond me. Meanwhile we're bailees for presumably stolen property.'

'Stolen by Clement Addis, though.'

'Who's dead,' Willis said. 'I'm sorry about that, I really am. And I admired his guts. All the same, perhaps it's just as well. You can't prosecute a dead man.'

Russell didn't comment—not to a policeman. It struck him as sound police thinking, sound police ethics. Stolen property was recovered, the stealer dead, so the police could decently close the file. It was perfectly proper thinking for a man whose business was upholding the law (when, Russell remembered, concealing a smile, he wasn't bending it to oblige a friend) but it wasn't legitimate thinking for the Security Executive whose business lay on the periphery of politics, a world where men seldom stole but always cheated. Against a political background Addis's suicide closed no book. Clement Addis was dead but his firm was surviving—just. True, it mightn't be easy to establish the dead man's guilt; it mightn't be easy to establish that any member of it had had knowledge of what he had done, nor would the ordinary person, his property restored, the criminal dead, seriously consider trying to. But in the Executive's world the people weren't ordinary. They thought not of property first but in terms of power. . . . The threat of scandal against an ancient firm, the enormously powerful levers of commercial and social blackmail. . . . Charles Russell's face went suddenly hard. He muttered a tiny prayer of grace. He was genuinely thankful that he wasn't Geoffrey Addis.

But he said nothing of this to the Chief Superintendent; instead he nodded understandingly, dismissing the tiara. 'That gets us out of that—we hope.' He fingered George Willis's paper. 'Next item, please.'

'Take your pick, sir.'

'As you please. I see you know who brought the briefcase to Addis junior.'

'Yes,' Willis said, 'it was a girl you've met, Sheila Raden.'

'You're pulling my leg.' Russell was incredulous and sounded it.

'Saving your presence it's much too muscular.'

'But why should Sheila Raden want to blow her own safe?'

Willis held a large hand up. 'Before we come to that one may I put the question differently? Why should anyone want to blow a safe when there was nobody there to dip it, not even an attempt to have another person present? It doesn't make sense.'

'You have a point.'

'And one I can't answer. No stealing, not even a chance to look inside. That destroys any possible theory that the reason for the blowing could have been to find out what the safe contained.'

'Does it?' Charles Russell said. 'I wonder.'

'I don't think I follow, sir.'

'I agree there's no basis for thinking that the safe was blown to discover what was in it. I'm less certain that it wasn't blown to find out what *wasn't* in it.'

George Willis shook his heavy head. 'I'm simply not with you.'

'Then forgive me if I think a bit.'

Charles Russell proceeded to do so. He'd been talking to Harry Tuke again and the Minister, now, was really worried. Russell thought he had reason to be so since an ordinary man or woman would have thought his position untenable. He wanted it both ways but politicians always did. His government wanted Shahbaddin as an uncommitted but friendly state, which it almost certainly wouldn't be if once the Chinese got the upper hand, but it didn't dare lean too openly towards the other half of two restless, uneasy bedfellows. In any case the favoured half were a dubious people to lean on. They had the defects of old hands in a pinch which they hadn't prepared for, and if they couldn't be changed the Chinese would win. When bang would go the paper balance, and with it any shaky pretence that the state was independent. What Harry Tuke really needed was an effective Malay alternative to a collection of ageing has-beens. And it didn't yet exist, neither the party nor the man. All there was were loose rumours of a man who'd been a soldier, then a professor in the university; he was a Malay they called simply Sayed, still whispering the name

79

behind lifted hands, but he'd vanished and gone underground. It was said he had some real support, even followers in England, and it wasn't inconceivable that he'd sent this Raden-Kendry to keep in touch.

But that wouldn't relieve an embarrassed British government, indeed the reverse. The High Commissioner would protest at once at the slightest hint of support to an underground party. Look how he'd raised the roof about this silly Raden jewellery, demanding official backing in what was clearly a private suit. And no British government could back a man in hiding, one it knew only by part of his name. In any case, what was a party without money and organization?

Money—the Raden jewels. They were perhaps not so silly. At least the High Commissioner had got a case on its feet to possess them. Ostensibly he was acting in the name of the whole of his government, but it was known that his office was as split as his country. Had His Excellency, a Malay, sold out quietly to the Chinese?

Charles Russell considered it, for it was an interesting hypothesis. It would explain quite a lot, but not, he decided, everything. The government of Shahbaddin was an unstable alliance of Malay and Chinese, but if the two had an interest in common it would be a distaste for losing power to any third. Money was the roots of power for any man or effective party, so the Raden case could be perfectly straightforward, a simple and mutual insurance that the jewels didn't subsidize a man or a party which could be dangerous if it possessed them.

Charles Russell thought it neat but insufficient: the logic stood up but the premises were inadequate. For they were inadequate by sheer value. . . . Fifty thousand pounds' worth odd of Raden family jewellery? It would be chicken feed to a political party. It wouldn't pay soldiers and far less arm them; it wouldn't subvert the police nor the state's machine.

No, but gold would. Gold—the yellow thing. The almost wholly useless, the almost all-powerful yellow stuff.

Charles Russell looked up at the Chief Superintendent. He was showing no signs of impatience yet but nor was Russell quite ready to talk. He gave the Chief Super a very dark whisky, murmuring an apology about getting his thoughts straight. In fact they were almost formed.

Gold. He had heard it from a journalist and apparently Harry Tuke hadn't. Nor was that remarkable. What Tuke received on Shahbaddin when he didn't insist on better was copied telegrams from the Foreign Office, absurdly marked Top Secret since they were a hotch-potch of gossip and cock-tail party behind-the-hands, an expensive collection of rubbish from airy-fairy and amateur sources. But this journalist had been different because he hadn't any axe to grind, no seniors to feed carefully on what you believed they would want to hear. And a rumour was sweeping Shahbaddin that the Radens had been hoarding gold, that for more than a generation they'd been stealing public moneys and salting them away in good gold bars. If that were true or even believed it would explain the urgency, even the violence, which a handful of family jewels did not. It was guessing of course, but worth trying on patient Willis.

'I'm sorry to have been rude. We left it, I think, on a some-what Delphic remark of mine. I was saying I thought it possible that the safe had been blown to discover what wasn't in it.'

'And I was saying I didn't follow.'

'Quite. Now tell me something about gold.'

'Gold, sir?' It wasn't the first time Charles Russell had surprised the police.

'Yes, bullion. You can't just keep it, can you? Working jewellers are allowed a bit but a private person can't sit on it. He has to offer it for sale under one of the regulations about exchange control.'

'Yes, that's right.'

'So if gold in any quantity had been found in the Raden safe then Mastertons, though jewellers, would have had to tender it promptly.'

'But it wasn't found in the Raden safe.'

'Precisely my point for what it's worth. There was nobody

there when the safe went up, but if gold had been inside it Mastertons would have sent it away. Which means armoured vans in the street, the whole damned circus.'

Willis said thoughtfully: 'Which anybody could have watched for and noticed if they were there.' He straightened up suddenly. 'Or not noticed if they didn't come.'

'Just so.'

'I must say, sir, you think of things.' George Willis was sounding sceptical.

'It's a negative bit of reasoning which I've been taught to mistrust as you have too. It don't press it in any way. But I do tell you this for what it's worth. It's widely believed in Shahbaddin that the Radens have a hoard of gold.'

'Is it indeed? I didn't know that.' Willis still sounded doubtful but he wasn't now openly sceptical; he scratched his chin, thinking, for Russell had hooked him; at last he said: 'In which case I'd like to ask you some questions. Starting with Miss Raden.'

'Yes, it's time we came back to Miss Raden.'

'Then wouldn't she have known if there'd been gold in that safe?'

'Perhaps. But her father was murdered and she's still a young woman.'

'So far we've been assuming that she acted for somebody else, somehow persuading young Addis to take in that briefcase. It isn't upper-class form to go bombing-up safes for amusement alone. Also she's not a technician at blowing them.'

'Nor is Oliver Kendry, alias Oliver Raden.'

'Who's he?'

'It's high time I told you. He's on the political side, the side you were trying to help me with. He's an illegitimate Raden, as it happens Miss Raden's cousin, and his mother was a Malay. He's over here now and I've put a shadow fairly close to him.' Charles Russell waved a deprecatory hand. 'Nothing very serious—not by your standards. But I'm interested in him politically which means I'm interested in his contacts. Little more than that just yet. You could call it a precaution which I've been asked to take and have. You could also guess by whom and why.'

Russell had been deprecatory but George Willis was clearly interested. 'He's half a Malay, I think you said. And you've been watching his contacts?'

'And got nowhere for the trouble. They're mostly students or cooks in restaurants, nothing sinister politically. One of them works in a garage.'

'A garage?' George Willis had risen suddenly, breathing hard.

'I'll give you a list.' Russell opened a drawer and passed it over. George Willis shook his head three times but at the fourth name froze like a pointer. 'Is the fourth man here the one at the garage?'

'Show me . . . Yes.'

'Have you checked on his past life?'

'Should I?'

'No—because I know it.' Willis swallowed but sat down. 'This man,' he said slowly, 'has done much time. He's a criminal, a safe-blower.'

'Interesting. Decidedly.' Russell was urbane still though privately he'd been shaken. 'Your side of the table that, I think.'

'I'll say.' George Willis was on his feet again, waving Charles Russell's list. In a man less disciplined the gesture would have been impertinent; he almost shook it in Russell's face; he said ominously: 'I'm going to recap.'

'Please do. I could use it.'

'So this is a list of your friend Raden's contacts?'

'Correct.'

'The first name is Sheila Raden?'

'Correct again.'

'And the fourth is a well-known peterman?'

'So you tell me.'

'My God,' Willis said, 'it's the oddest one in a copper's life.'

'Sit down, my dear chap—relax. We're in this together and I don't like it a bit.'

This Willis ignored. 'We've questioned Sheila Raden of course.'

'And what did she say?'

A very strange look crossed George Willis's face, a compound of irritation and a real but reluctant respect. 'She gave us a voluntary statement. There was no sort of pressure since that's always unwise unless you're prepared to hold somebody. Which we were not. A Miss Raden is a Miss Raden—quite a lot stands behind her. But she admitted at once that she'd handed in the briefcase, so we asked her if she knew what it contained. Naturally she said she didn't. A friend had asked her to deliver it—just like that. Then we asked her what friend and do you know what she said?' It was a rhetorical question and Russell disliked them. Willis had to answer himself. 'She said she'd think that over and let us know. By God, she's a cool one.'

'That was my own impression of Sheila Raden.'

'You can't help admiring them, the genuine thoroughbreds.' Willis looked at his watch. 'I'm going to snatch a sandwich and a beer. I've another appointment with Miss Raden at two o'clock. She said she'd come back and I don't doubt she will.'

'Let me know what she says.'

'I will.'

Russell saw George Willis out and walked down to his club for luncheon. When he came back there was a message on his desk. Chief Superintendent Willis had telephoned and would be grateful if Colonel Russell would ring back. Russell promptly did so.

'Willis? She's told you where she got the thing?'

There was a long embarrassed silence, then Willis's voice *piano*. 'Next to bribery and a scandal there's just one thing a good policeman hates. That's poking about in embassies, questioning the diplomats. . . .'

He rung off abruptly.

Oliver Raden was waiting for Sheila's return. He was in her

flat and had guessed that it was unwise to be but he hadn't been able to keep away. For Oliver Raden was sorely ashamed, pacing the duplex wretchedly, wrestling with a sickness. A Christian would have diagnosed it as a case of suspended conscience. He hadn't, he thought, had the right to do it, not to commit her half in ignorance. It was true that she'd helped him voluntarily: he'd warned her that they could jail her and she'd gone to Mastertons almost gaily. True. But would she have gone if he'd come out with it unequivocally, that it was gold which was his quarry not a safeload of family trinkets, gold as the sinews of a new political party? It had ruthless and powerful enemies—his hands told him that still—and anyone who helped it could be equally in danger. It hadn't been just to expose her in partial ignorance; it hadn't been just to a cousin by blood and it hadn't been just to the woman he wanted. He felt as stricken as a catholic obsessed by a bout of original sin.

When Sheila came in he jumped to meet her. 'How did the interview go?'

She seemed perfectly collected and he wished he had it too. 'I think it went fairly well,' she said.

'The police pressed you for where you got it of course?'

'They pressed me all right but they didn't put their claws out. Not that they haven't got them. That could come later.'

'What did you say?'

'I gave them a name.'

His lean face fell though he tried to control it. It had been part of their understanding and without it he wouldn't have let her go. If she got into serious trouble she was to tell the truth at once; she was to give the police Oliver Raden's name.

'I see,' he said flatly. He didn't blame her, he couldn't.

'But I don't think you do. I gave them a name but it wasn't yours. I told them I got it from a man in the High Commissioner's.'

He stared at her unbelieving.

'It seemed a pretty good idea. I told them it was something he wanted included in the lawsuit and that I'd agreed to do it to save more legal fuss. I'm certain they didn't believe me but they couldn't disprove it there and then.' She looked at him. 'Can you?'

He didn't answer the question. 'But you don't know anybody at the High Commissioner's office. You never go there.'

'I don't—it stinks. But I met a man at a party once. I remembered his name.'

'Who was that?'

'Mr Kin.'

For a moment he was silent, then began to laugh enormously. She hadn't known he could laugh like that and she loved him more hotly for it. She'd thought of him as too scholarly, too reserved, too controlled and dry, but he was sitting before her helpless now, holding his flat stomach with his hands in those horrible gloves of his, the uninhibited rictus of his face the classical mask of laughter. She thought he was going to choke and brought him water. He waved it away and slowly cooled. At last he said:

'You told them it was Mr Kin? Mr Kin who gave you the briefcase?'

'That's what I said.'

'It was a really outrageous lie, you know.'

'It didn't seem a bad one at the time.' She sounded surprised, a little puzzled.

He began to laugh again but checked it. 'It will keep the police quiet for a day at least. Questioning diplomats is a very tricky business for a policeman. They're bound to find out in the end but you've bought us time.'

'Time for what?'

'Come here,' he said. 'I'll tell you.'

She sat on his lap for perhaps twenty minutes; she listened in total silence and then got up.

'I ought to have told you before,' he said. 'I ought to have told you everything.'

She entirely ignored it. 'So they tortured you for the gold,' she said. 'Does it exist?'

'I don't know. A friend of mine watched at Mastertons and

86

it didn't come out of there. But I've been sent to find out. To get it if I can as well.'

'And the Chinese want it?'

'Kin especially. But what really concerns them is that *we* shouldn't have it. It might mean little to them but it means everything to us, even arms if it comes to a fight which I hope it won't. It needn't if we have money.' He looked at her, misreading her face. 'I ought to have told you,' he said again.

'I don't see why. It's reasonable to test people.'

'I wasn't doing that.'

'Perhaps.' She gave him a smile which had him instantly on his feet. Against his shoulder, when he would let her, she asked at last: 'Did I pass the test? I'm with you, you know. I want to be. I must.'

'It's dangerous,' he said foolishly. 'The English police——'

She said something dismissive about the excellent British police.

'Just the same, a false statement—that's serious in England.'

'And what makes you think I'll be staying in England?'

This time they both laughed.

CHAPTER SEVEN

Mr Kin was depressed, trying to convince himself that he had no real reason to be so. It wasn't as though he were some pawn to be pushed around, some third-rate agent to die dirtily in Berlin. He'd been thoroughly trained and remorselessly indoctrinated and now he stood quite high in a potent hierarchy. He had an international organization which would accept his orders; he didn't precisely control it but it would take his instructions, and if he suspected that once or twice it had referred them upwards before complying, then so far at least they had never been countermanded. It was an organization which reached everywhere, dedicated and ruthless, and in England few even guessed its power. The Security Executive could do more than guess—it knew; but Charles Russell was often hamstrung by the laughable British system of law. And behind the organization stood a brutally resurgent state. No, Kin decided, he hadn't good cause to feel depressed simply because his latest instructions had been more tersely phrased than usual.

He had decoded them himself since there was nobody else who could do so, and now he took them from his safe. They hadn't come from Shahbaddin but from considerably east of it. Kin had read them several times already but now did so again, his smooth face hardening. The tone was severe and even minatory. Kin's masters were worried.

. . . This man Sayed could be more dangerous than had originally been supposed. It was true he was underground still, but he'd been sufficiently well-organized to rescue Oliver Raden at gunpoint and later to send him to England. Why? That could only be in connection with the Raden gold, for who could better find it than the Radens?

Of whom two were now in England.

That wouldn't do, it wouldn't indeed. Raden sympathies were officially neutral but they certainly weren't pro-Chinese. So there was an obvious neo-colonialist plot—the Raden gold in Sayed's hands in return for the restoration of ancient privileges in some new form. And that could be far from some exile's dream since with gold in his hands Sayed could be formidable. Gold bought arms, bought men, the police. . . . Three years of intensive work brought to nothing, for they were now very close, as Kin would know. The present government was crumbling, almost gone; many of its leaders were already secretly foresworn, and in the last few days Kin's own High Commissioner had finally come over. The only development which could wreck the years of planning would be some sudden new opposition, an instinctive indigenous rising under a man who would know how to use it. Sayed, for instance— he had the drive. But not without gold the sinews of war. Agreed? And the gold must be in England. But so was Mr Kin. That was clear?

Mr Kin decided grimly that it was very clear indeed. For a moment his depression returned; he fought it off. Still, it wasn't the morning he'd have chosen to talk to a policeman. He'd have to of course, he couldn't refuse.

He'd seen a line or two in the evening papers, fuller reports in the dailies this morning. There'd been a safeblowing at Mastertons and at a firm of that eminence that was news in its own right, though a long way from a front page spread in a day and an age when organized crime was a flourishing industry. But this morning two newspapers had linked the blown safe with the fact that an injunction had been running on it, one granted at the instance of Mr Kin's own High Commissioner. The stories, if you called them that, had been cagy to the extreme, bare statements of the connection and little else. Kin had nodded understandingly. Even hint the dread words *sub judice* to any British editor and at once he'd clap the brakes on, but the police would have their duty still and they'd be making their lawful inquiries. On the ladder of his office Kin wasn't the natural man to call on first, but he'd been to Mastertons personally so no doubt they'd have given the police his name. Though hardly, he knew, the purpose of his visit. Mastertons were now in an embarrassing situation and they'd scarcely wish to complicate it by allegations of attempted bribery which they hadn't a hope of making stick. Geoffrey Addis hadn't co-operated but he hadn't seemed stupid either.

So Mr Kin received the Inspector of Police with a cool and casual courtesy. The Inspector for his part had a difficult mission, and he was experienced enough to have covered himself by taking careful, express instructions. He began on a note of almost stylized routine. Mr Kin would have heard that the Raden safe at Mastertons had been blown the previous afternoon, and that safe had been covered by an injunction applied for by Mr Kin's High Commissioner. So a call by the police had been necessary.

Kin had nodded again, waiting.

There were one or two curious features. First, nothing had been taken. Nothing *could* have been taken. The circumstances were unusual in that there had been no attempt to steal, indeed the blowing had been so organized that no stealing had been possible. Could Kin throw any light on that? Even comment might be helpful.

He had shaken his head but asked at once: 'And how was the blowing done?'

Ah, that was the second oddity. There'd been a charge of explosives contained in a leather briefcase which Mr Addis junior had been asked to put into the safe a matter of minutes before the actual explosion. There was some doubt about that action, whether or not it was a breach of the undertaking, but as the Inspector was advised on it there was at least a *prima facie* case that technically it might not be. In any case that was a matter of civil law, at any rate for the moment, and civil law was outside police competence.

Kin was silent. He thought this was shameful rubbish, a shocking bourgeois indifference to the paramount rights of the state, but he'd been thoroughly trained before they'd posted him to London and his training had included the proper attitude to English law. One was entitled to despise it but it was very unwise to display one's contempt. He shared this thought, though he didn't know it, with that rising young solicitor David Marks.

But he'd also been trained to listen, to ask a question as well when he had to, and now he asked the important one.

'Who asked Mr Addis to put that briefcase in the Raden safe?'

The Inspector seemed to hesitate; he'd hesitated because it was awkward. It wasn't normal practice to pass on statements to a third party, but this one had included a definite allegation against the third party in question. He'd taken his careful, express instructions, but nevertheless he approached his first fence cautiously.

'The briefcase,' he said, 'was handed over by Sheila Raden. Of course that's confidential.'

For a second Kin's bland face broke. . . . The Radens! So the Radens were in this openly now. They *had* gone in with Sayed, they were after it too. . . .

He recovered himself at once. 'But why did she do that?'

'We don't know that yet.'

'But you will?'

'We're pursuing our inquiries,' the Inspector said formally. He'd expected to be pressed and was experienced at resisting pressure.

'I don't want to seem to be interfering, but I should have thought there was an obvious line. Explosives, I mean, and an apparently respectable young woman. Her motive apart, where did she get them?'

'Rest assured we're following that one.' The Inspector hesitated again. This was the real jump and he'd have to face it; he said at length: 'Unfortunately there's another line.'

'Unfortunately?'

'It gives us some difficulty. The young lady made a state-ment as to where she got the briefcase.'

'Then surely——'

'In any normal circumstances we'd have followed that up gladly. But as things stand she merely embarrassed us.'

'But she gave you a name?'

'She did. It was yours.'

For a moment the Inspector feared that Kin was going to strike him. He had risen and was choking. The Inspector watched him impassively. . . . What colour did the Chinese go when they were under strong emotion. They were yellowish to start with. White? Brick colour? Purple? Kin's colour hadn't changed much so the question went unanswered, but the Inspector had seen many shocked men and this one was up with the leaders. It would be awkward if he struck him but the Inspector didn't believe he would. He was fighting himself and slowly winning.

At last Kin sat down. He said, not quite clearly: 'You believe this preposterous story?'

'No.'

'Then why do you tell me?'

The Inspector said peaceably: 'We have to have your formal denial.'

'You have it.'

'Thank you.' The Inspector rose. 'I don't think I need trouble you more today. Naturally we'll be keeping in touch.' He walked out quickly but composedly since he didn't want further questions.

When he had gone Kin poured an enormous whisky. He didn't drink often but now he swallowed the spirit neat. He took his orders from the safe again.

. . . Bad. Bad for Kin. There was no mistaking the import of the plain statement that Kin was in England. He was being held responsible and he'd have to produce results or else.

He began to consider the possibilities. Go directly for Sheila Raden? He would gladly have seen her dead. What she'd done was an impertinence, an insult to him personally and to a dedicated man a gay cocking of a snook at the coldly serious world he worked for. He'd have happily seen her dead or worse, or perhaps there were ways to squeeze her. But Kin shook his head. Sheila dead would not advance him. To kill her would be a concession to personal feeling and he'd been taught that that was the final sin. Even to try to blackmail the girl would have its own unacceptable risks. For she wasn't some wretched nonentity, scared and already half broken. Sheila Raden was Sheila Raden, the daughter of a His Highness, an upper-class young Englishwoman on her own and still formidable ground. The least hint of trouble and she'd know where to go. Not to the police—a Raden could do better than that. She'd have friends and connections and she could reach where it mattered. Mr Kin knew his England or considered that he did so and he smiled a little dourly. He'd just remembered that Miss Raden knew Colonel Russell. He'd seen them talking at a party, and people who knew Charles Russell could be unattractive targets. So he'd leave her alone but he'd have her discreetly watched. Someday she might lead them on to it or at least give a line to where it was.

He picked up a telephone and gave quick orders in Chinese.

And then there was Geoffrey Addis. . . . Better. There were possibilities there in the classic mould—blackmail, intolerably increasing pressure. That policeman hadn't said much, but Mastertons must be in an awkward spot. A safe with an injunction on it, and under their noses the safe gets blown. They'd been parties to the blowing too, or rather it wouldn't have happened if Geoffrey Addis hadn't known Sheila. That opened up another line and Kin considered it seriously. He'd heard that Geoffrey Addis had been courting Sheila Raden, and if that were true he wouldn't be pleased. Kin smiled again at the understatement: he'd have been made to look a perfect fool by a woman he wanted to marry. Excellent. The English pose was to despise the vendetta, but many men and women had been broken mistaking the convention for reality. The English had their own cool pride and it was dangerous to affront it, more dangerous than the stranger knew since the English were a patient race and one trained from childhood to hide its real feelings. Geoffrey wouldn't forget a humiliation, Kin was sure he wasn't the type to, and if by some strange chance he tried, well, there were other pressures. There was something fishy about Mastertons. Kin had heard the rumours since it was part of his trade to hear things. And why had old Addis blown out his brains? That had been in the papers too. Shame for the house of Mastertons getting done? No, hardly enough for suicide. So it came down to this and to Kin it looked promising: Geoffrey Addis might wish to co-operate or if he didn't he could be made to.

Kin picked up another telephone and gave further sharp instructions. He wanted information about Mastertons and its background. Proof was irrelevant, he wasn't interested in the lawsuit now. He wanted the story, he wanted the dirt. Dirt could stick and be used and he intended to use it.

He put down the telephone, and this time he was looking pleased. Though he hadn't an idea of it he was sharing an Englishman's thought again, Charles Russell's opinion that Geoffrey Addis was very vulnerable.

But there was still a matter to be decided—Oliver Raden. Kin had good reason to take him seriously. It was an almost certain guess that he'd stood behind Sheila in blowing the safe, and it was known that Sayed had sent him here; he was the agent in England of a man Kin's masters increasingly feared and clearly he was the essential brains in any plan to discover and snatch the gold. So Raden must be eliminated and that action *was* perfectly possible. The girl was too established to touch but Oliver Raden wasn't. For one thing he wasn't a Raden in name, and even if he had been he hadn't been here for long enough to form the connections which put Sheila out of Kin's long reach. On the contrary he was lying low, from Kin's latest instructions almost in hiding. He had friends and some contacts but none of them were important ones. It would be logical to eliminate him and it was within Kin's power to do so.

Kin decided to tell the High Commissioner. There was malice in this since he needn't pay further attention to a man who was now a stooge, but Kin despised his High Commissioner and it amused him to see him wriggle. He had recently made his choice—the Chinese would win—and now he must take orders from Mr Kin. He also knew where they came from and that wasn't from his government, but His Excellency had a mistress in Shepherd's Bush and a club in Pall Mall he was greatly attached to. Life in England he found congenial and they'd promised to leave him in London.

He'd sold out and Kin despised him, but he offered him the courtesies still, walking along the corridor, knocking politely and waiting to hear 'Come in'. He waited, too, to be asked to sit down. The invitation came too quickly and Kin noticed it sardonically. But his voice was a nominal junior's still as he put what in fact was already a decision.

'I'd be grateful for Your Excellency's advice in the matter of Oliver Raden.'

'Yes, I knew he was here. Using the name of Kendry, I think.'

'I don't think that's important.'

'Perhaps you're right.' There was a considerable, an uneasy pause before His Excellency added: 'Well?'

'It's been decided he must go.'

'Leave the country, you mean? You think we could arrange——'

'Not leave the country.'

'Then?'

'It's been decided he must be eliminated.'

The High Commissioner said weakly: 'Liquidated?' He was learning the language.

'Just so.'

For a moment Kin thought he was going to show fight, for a second the man was angry. Kin watched his face with a clinical detachment. First the flicker of anger, then the doubt and the knowledge of impotence. His Excellency was powerless now, His Excellency knew it. He covered his face with his hands and through them said:

'Go away. Please go away.'

Mr Kin went away. He would indulge a certain malice but

he wasn't a simple sadist. It would have given him no pleasure to see his High Commissioner weeping.

Back in his office he used the telephone again. He was speaking now in English, and when he had finished the telephone whistled.

'A tall order,' it said.

'But still an order.'

'I know.' There was a thoughtful pause. 'How long have I got?'

'Twenty-four hours would suit me. We can't afford more.'

The voice said: 'Can do.'

Sheila and Oliver Raden had parted laughing, but in the Security Executive Charles Russell was not. He had half a lifetime of experience of the sort of situation where Ministers told you to do something but seldom what, and it wasn't unknown for inaction to be by far the wisest course. But his instinct this morning was that there was more to this affair than simply a Minister's nervousness. He had been reading some fresh reports from Shahbaddin, talking again to his journalist friend, putting that background against his chat with Chief Superintendent Willis. Willis was interested in what was ostensibly a non-political crime, but there was a strongly suggestive thread between the safeblowing and the Radens. Who inescapably smelt of politics. Willis would work on the case as crime and from what Russell gathered he was already in deep waters. That meant more time, and though delay could be helpful it could also be dangerous. On the political side, that is—the Raden side. The threads were still unravelled but such as they were led clearly to Oliver Raden. And that aspect was purest politics, international ones at that. It was a different world from Willis's, less predictable and more ruthless. Russell was there to read it or when he couldn't to guess wisely. He was guessing at this moment though he wouldn't have called it wisely; he would have said instead, modestly, that insurance could do no harm.

He picked up a telephone and asked for Mrs Maguffy. He

smiled contentedly as he waited since Mary Maguffy was a very good friend. She was a deceptively comfortable-looking woman of maybe forty, the wife of a C.I.D. sergeant whom she couldn't contrive to live with. Nor he with her. A week in a matrimonial home and life became immediate hell. But if they couldn't share a house together nor could they live entirely apart, so once a month and sometimes more they went off for a long weekend. To Brighton, to Southend, and sometimes, when they were flush, to Rome. Charles Russell knew this but the sergeant's superiors didn't. Russell had never told them. He didn't think it his business and he was scrupulous in minding that. In any case he considered it a most civilized arrangement.

Mary Maguffy was also one of his short-list operators.

When she came through Charles Russell asked her: 'Have you heard of Oliver Raden?'

'The name rings a bell.'

'What sort of bell?'

'Not Oliver Raden but Sheila. There was some sort of safe-breaking and perhaps Sheila Raden——'

Russell said sharply: 'Her name hasn't been in the papers yet. Where did you pick up that bit?'

'I sometimes talk to policemen, you know.' The placid contralto voice was undisturbed.

'Sergeants in the C.I.D. should never gossip.' Russell was speaking with such severity as he could muster. It wasn't entirely convincing since he was struggling with a smile as well.

'But they do, you know. To their wives when they can trust them.'

'Maguffy's under Willis, I think.'

'That's right.'

'I see. . . . Did you both have a nice weekend?'

'Splendid, thank you,' she said politely.

'Good. But forget about Sheila Raden. I want Oliver Raden protected.'

'Against what?'

'The usual things. I've got a man on him already but he's

only a shadow—Raden's movements and his contacts but so far nothing more. Now I have reason to fear for him and that means an operator. So I'll take the shadow off and leave Raden to you.'

'And how do I clue up on him?'

Russell looked at his watch which showed a quarter-past ten. 'The file will be in your usual drop by eleven o'clock at latest.'

'I understand.'

'Any questions?'

'Yes, I have. What do I do if this Raden gets into trouble?'

'You get him out of it of course.'

'And afterwards?'

'You take him or what's left of him to Sheila Raden's flat. You don't need any briefing on her and the address is in the directory.'

'May I ask why?'

'Of course you may.' Russell considered, then began to spell it out. 'There's some sort of connection between Sheila Raden and this Oliver, I mean beyond the fact that they're natural cousins. On the face of it they were both mixed up in the safe-blowing you were gossiping about. Willis is looking after that, but I'm inclined to think there's something more and you could call it something political.'

'How does dumping him at Sheila's place help? I ought to know what to watch for.'

'Watch for how she takes the dumping, watch for how she receives the unexpected guest. If she simply asks "What's happened" and "Who are you?" then we shan't be any further. But I've a hunch that she's much closer to him than that. So if she takes him in as a matter of course, if she grabs him from the stranger, bangs the door in your face——'

'I'll put my foot in and ask some awkward ones.'

'You will do no such foolishness. You wouldn't get worth-while answers. But if she takes him in unquestioningly we'll know a little more where we are. Also where *they* are—physically. *Both* of them. Two for the price of one and I'm short of good people. So if it breaks that way you can stay around the pair of them. Report to me first though, that goes without saying. Any more questions?'

'No sir.'

'Good hunting.'

Russell rang off and Maguffy hung up. Her rich contralto made a comment but an affectionate one.

'Cunning old bastard,' Mary said.

CHAPTER EIGHT

Oliver Raden was fastidious about food but in England had grown indifferent. He could find neither good rice nor the sort of fruit he fancied, and since the flesh of the pig was forbidden by his religion he had to be careful with casual snacks. He was inclined to eat where he could see what he was eating, and the sandwiches at the Stag were at least freshly cut. More important, when they said 'Beef' they were. He was sitting this evening at the elaborate Victorian bar, eating beef sandwiches and drinking orange squash. This wasn't resented since he'd been accepted at the Stag. It was a respectable mostly middle-class pub and Oliver suited its ambience; he answered politely when spoken to but he never accosted strangers first; he ate quickly and tidily and he always tipped the barman but not too much.

At a table in the corner a comfortable-looking woman of maybe forty was watching him without seeming to. Behind her second Guinness Mary Maguffy was thinking. She had picked up her brief from her drop and had read it carefully. There'd been a photograph too but the reality had surprised her. She'd read that Oliver Raden was half Malay but she wouldn't have guessed it from sight of him alone; she'd have put him as a foreigner, an Italian perhaps though not the comic opera kind, neither greasy nor stout but lean and taut. A foreigner yes, but never what was intolerably miscalled a half caste. Mary Maguffy found him powerfully attractive, and the attraction returned a line of thought she'd already travelled.

Which was what was Charles Russell playing at? You could never be quite sure of that however well you believed you knew him. Mary knew him intimately, not in his bed since he'd never asked her (he wouldn't, she thought smiling, since he kept his own rules) but with the comfortable unassuming ease of people with values in common, though she'd been working for him for a year at least before they'd unexpectedly but finally meshed. He had asked her to the theatre, a mark of approval he sometimes paid, and Mary Maguffy had accepted it as such. But afterwards there'd been taxi-trouble and Russell had insisted that he escort her home by tube. And suddenly, over nothing at all, they'd been friends of a lifetime's standing.

It had been nothing at all but quite enough. On the opposite seat two teenagers had been necking uninhibitedly and the woman on Russell's left had begun to mutter. Mary didn't hear all of it but caught 'Scandalous' and 'In public too'. She looked sideways at Charles Russell and his face was as red as a brick. Well, Mary thought, they were taking it rather far.

To her astonishment Russell spoke to the woman beside him. He took off his hat but he barked like a drill sergeant. 'Madam,' he said, 'you're talking nonsense.'

'I don't know who you think you are——'

'I'm a man knocking sixty and I mind my own business carefully. I suggest you do the same.'

'But it's a scandal——'

'Be quiet.'

Mary had never heard Russell rude, but clearly he was moved and she guessed a reason. This distinguished and elegant man was wholly human. Mary knew too that there were two conditioned reflexes to the sight of young people necking: one was scandalized and disgusted and the other longed to tuck them up. It wasn't a bad dividing line between the civilized and the barbarous. Charles Russell was clearly civilized and Mary began to play with it. . . . So if he hadn't a Scots housekeeper he might just possibly have invited them home. They'd probably steal his cigarettes and foul up his loo with bits of rubber; they might even fail to thank him when they sheepishly left next morning, but he'd treat them with formal courtesy proof against any boorishness. Mary Maguffy had wanted to laugh. Her thought had been a fantasy but it hadn't been quite a stupid one. She looked at Russell again and saw him smile. Then they began to laugh together on the best of shared jokes, the unspoken one, two happy and tolerant adults, or at least as happy as a world designed for savages allowed.

Mary thought of this now as she watched Oliver Raden. She had read her dossier carefully and there'd been a photograph of Sheila thrown in. Mary, a generous woman, had thought her beautiful. So she was to dump this virile man in the flat of that splendid girl. And then? It made administrative sense no doubt: if the girl took him in she could cope with them both, and it was true that Charles Russell was short of good operators. Two for the price of one, he'd said, and that was always tempting to the frugal administrator. Just the same she couldn't help wondering.

She stopped wondering abruptly as a man slid on to the stool at Oliver's side. Mary had been comprehensively trained, but it was instinct nor training which now raised her hackles. The man wasn't a rough but there was something about him. Mary couldn't have defined it but she was sure. If she hadn't been quite sure of it she'd have been just another number on the Executive's list of people it could give orders to but couldn't quite trust to act alone.

Mary Maguffy had never been that.

The man ordered a beer and took a solid pull at it, then tugged at a folded newspaper in the pocket of his raincoat. The newspaper seemed to be sticking and came out with an unexpected jerk. The man's arm flew up, the newspaper with it, and Oliver Raden's orange squash went over on the bar counter.

The man said fairly pleasantly: 'I'm sorry. I'll get you another.'

'That's kind but you shouldn't bother. There was almost none left.' Oliver pointed at the counter. There had indeed been almost nothing left and the barman was swabbing it casually.

The stranger's manner hardened. 'I don't think you're quite English,' he said.

'No, not quite.'

'But it's time you learnt our customs just the same. When you knock a man's drink down you buy him another.'

'But I don't want another one,' Oliver said politely.

'Are you trying to insult me?'

'Of course not.'

'Well, you are.'

The man had slipped off his stool and Mary rose. But she didn't yet move—the affair wasn't ripe. It wouldn't be a gun, she thought, and probably not even a knife. The man in the raincoat had the air that he knew his business. He was playing it for a scuffle and then he'd close.

Oliver Raden too had got down from his stool. 'I'm not trying to offend you.' He spoke quietly but not in apology.

'But you are.'

The barman said: 'Gentlemen——'

The stranger took a swing and missed and Mary Maguffy nodded. She didn't doubt his skill at all and a blow with the fist was the merest gambit. Oliver might hit back or move, somehow he'd offer the opening. . . .

He hadn't yet done so but he had taken off his spectacles. He stood waiting for the next blow to come, embarrassed but not afraid.

The other took two steps forward and Mary six. His right arm had gone round Oliver's waist, pulling his coat back, baring the kidney. His left hand was out on a rigid arm, not closed in a fist but sideways, deadly.

. . . He does know his stuff, he can maim, perhaps kill.

Mary kicked high at the tautened elbow. She showed a plump but shapely thigh in the act but on duty she wasn't conventional. As she moved her leg she shook her arm and the blackjack slipped down neatly from the sleeve-clip into her palm. She hit raincoat once at the base of the neck.

He fell like a stone.

Mary took Oliver's hand and pulled. 'Come on.'

He started to talk but she silenced him with authority. 'Come with me—we'll talk later.' The bar was in an uproar now and Mary wanted no part of it. 'Watch your step as we leave, there might be others.'

'Other what?'

'You'll find out if there are any.'

But they left the bar unmolested. Round the corner in a cul-de-sac was Mary's modest runabout. It was parked quite illegally but its number was recorded where it mattered. Mary led Oliver to it and opened the door.

'We're going for a little drive.'

He said on a note of polite inquiry: 'I don't think I have the pleasure——'

'I'm Mrs Mary Maguffy and I work for a Colonel Russell.'

'I've heard the name—who hasn't? The Security Executive, isn't it?'

'It is.'

He got into the car at once and Mary smiled. He was looking astonished but she was used to that. . . . A woman? But what did they expect, the clots? Some beautifully dressed young gentleman waving a gun when there wasn't a need to do so, or some nameless slick hoodlum from south of the river whom the Executive wouldn't have dreamt of taking on in a hundred years? They read far too many spy stories. Why, the blackjack apart she wasn't even armed. She didn't need to be armed for nine-tenths of the time and the tenth, if it looked like coming up, Charles Russell would mostly smother. Oliver had come quietly but it wouldn't have mattered to Mary if he had not. She weighed herself regularly, sometimes averting her eyes from the dial, but when you were a professional a half-stone wasn't important. She could have taken Oliver one-handed and if she'd had to would have done so.

She'd been piqued by his absurd surprise but now she was taking him in, approval rising. He'd asked only one question, 'Where are we going?' and she'd answered: 'To your cousin's flat.' Most men would have started yapping, but instead he'd shrugged, held a light to her cigarette. Her opinion of Oliver Raden mounted steadily. There would have to be explanations and she was ready to give them decently, but there was bound to be talk at Sheila's flat and she hated having to say it twice.

She stopped the car where he told her, this time parking legally, and they went up in the lift to Sheila's flat. Oliver rang and Sheila opened. Oliver said quickly, politely but with an undertone half of amusement, half of respect: 'This is Mary Maguffy of the Security Executive. I think you've met Charles Russell and she tells me that she works for him. I've no reason to doubt it at all.'

Sheila stared for a second but recovered herself at once. 'Won't you come in?'

Mary had feared a stream of questions but Oliver was avoiding them. On the journey he seemed to have worked it out and, since he'd got it right, she let him explain to Sheila.

'A man tried to pick a quarrel in a pub. I think I know who hired him and maybe you can guess. We'll talk about that later. It might have been very ugly indeed but Mrs Maguffy dealt with that.' His manner was dry but his voice was still respectful. 'She's a very effective woman.'

'Thank you,' Sheila Raden said. She was taking it with a steady calm, almost as though she'd expected some trouble. Mary Maguffy observed it with interest.

She returned to them from her private thoughts. Since Raden was doing the talking she'd let him talk, looking round the flat instead, taking it in a sharp inspection. It was a duplex and the bed was in the gallery. It wasn't quite a double bed but would hold more than one quite comfortably. There was also a sofa downstairs but not a big one. Mary noticed both amiably. Like Charles Russell she wasn't a prude.

Sheila was saying warmly: 'Can I give you a drink? We don't drink ourselves but I've got some whisky.'

Mary noted the 'we' and accepted the whisky. Oliver gave her a generous shot, a smaller smile. 'I knew I had friends here or I wouldn't have come. But it seems that I've got more than I knew and they're most efficient.'

'Colonel Russell can be a helpful friend.'

'If I could ask his motive, why he's interested in me at all . . .?'

She shook her head.

He didn't appear annoyed or offended, accepting it without comment. 'But I can ask for your advice perhaps.'

'Well, somebody's trying to get you and you seem to know who it is. That's never good.'

'How bad? I had my glasses off. You saw it and I didn't see much.'

'He could have maimed you and he meant to. Perhaps he would have tried to kill.'

She heard Sheila stifle a sudden sound but when she looked at her quickly Sheila was silent. She seemed to be thinking, then said with decision:

'In that case Mr Raden stays here.'

'It mightn't be a bad idea but don't spoil it by taking half-measures. Don't let him go out. If you intend to keep him *keep* him.' Mary rose and Oliver with her. Her job was over for the moment except for the call to Russell. Oliver held the door for her. 'I've got to thank you for quite a lot,' he said.

'For nothing. I'll stick around till I'm taken off. Good-night.'

'Goodnight.'

In the passage outside the duplex Mary Maguffy lit a reflective cigarette. She nodded again approvingly. . . . A beautiful girl and a man who most certainly was one. Mary Maguffy was happy for the pair of them.

She was happy but on duty still, and as she left the block of duplexes she froze. Across the road in a shadow a man had been standing quietly but as Mary came out he began to move. She wasn't astonished. Russell hadn't told her everything yet but Sheila and Oliver Raden were connected in some affair he thought was dangerous. So if Mary's job was to watch on Oliver somebody else could be watching Sheila. It wouldn't be one of Russell's or he'd have told her.

Interesting. Well worth verifying.

She followed the man smoothly, keeping her distance but running no risk of losing him, accelerating when he did. She wasn't yet sure but soon she would be. They crossed the

King's Road, walking steadily north. The man dived suddenly into a public lavatory.

The oldest trick in the book and not the best.

At the head of the steps was the civic euphemism GENTLEMEN, but Mary didn't hesitate. There was an immediate protest from an acneous youth, one very much more dignified from a uniformed Chelsea Pensioner. Mary paid no attention. At the end of the busy line was a hat and a figure she recognized. Now she could see that the man was a Chinese. Next to him was a vacant place and Mary stepped into it briskly.

The Chelsea Pensioner said despairingly: 'Not that.'

Mary was watching fascinated. . . . So that was yellowish too, she'd often wondered. More important, could he use it? If he could it would tell her nothing but if he couldn't she would be certain. He'd have come in here to lose her and he'd have only one motive for doing that. She'd *know*.

She gave him ten seconds, then a sibilant encouraging hiss. The Chinese swore.

'Potty-potty. Good boy.'

The Chinese cursed but the Chinese gave up. Mary patted him on the shoulder. 'You're not very good at your job,' she said.

CHAPTER NINE

M r Kin had made contact with Geoffrey Addis again by the straightforward method of walking into Mastertons and asking for him. But he had thought very carefully before doing so.

He had good reason to think carefully since his instructions, now arriving almost daily, were a steady crescendo of urgency. This morning's, for instance, had been issued in the name of a man he had never met, one outside the organization he worked for, not quite the highest in the land but unquestionably in a position to give orders to Kin's own superiors. Who had attempted no softening of the bleak outlines of their message, no whitewash on what they told him was a situation growing serious.

For the man they called Sayed had more support than had been supposed; he now had a popular grassroots grip which an able man could always exploit, perhaps as organized non-co-operation, perhaps even as active disturbances. The state was sick and the people restless, and that was the classic backdrop for the emergence of the man on the big white horse. Not that Sayed had the horse yet, or in terms of Shahbaddin the armoured cars, but the police couldn't be relied on if it came to an open showdown. On the contrary they were wavering, and certain officials behind them were wavering too. Kin's master's own bid for power was almost ripe, but if Sayed struck first he had a very real chance.

He'd have a better with two million pounds—that was the latest estimate of the gold which the Radens had stolen and salted away. It would naturally be in England, and so at this moment were two of the Radens. As was Kin himself, and with authority and resources. That had been said before but must now be repeated. His local power was unquestioned but so was his responsibility. If he wanted it in specific terms it must be put like this and in no other way: to obtain the gold would be straight success, provided only that it was done promptly and if possible without scandal. And successes were never forgotten. But if that were impracticable the second best must be accepted, the certainty that at least Sayed should never lay hands on what Kin could not. That wouldn't be success but nor would it be accounted total failure.

And total failures were never forgotten either.

Kin considered these orders with the gravity they deserved, deciding, though not too certainly, that it would still be premature to accept the second best. The Raden gold could still be secured rather than merely neutralized. There was the minimum of time but three self-evident possibilities. True. But abstract possibilities were something he'd learnt from long experience to mistrust, and now he began to translate them into terms of the living people.

First Sheila Raden. Whom he'd already decided to let alone, and now he had better reason still for leaving her on the loosest rein, a continuing watch on her movements but nothing more. For Sheila Raden would be in trouble of her own making. The least hint of pressure from Mr Kin and the girl had powerful friends she could call in aid, but they weren't so powerful, or not in England, that they could protect her from a breach of the ordinary law. Which she'd inescapably committed. She'd put an explosive briefcase into the family safe at Mastertons, then told an impertinent lie to the police. They hadn't believed her, they'd told Kin that, and they'd hardly suppose she had made the bomb herself. So they'd probe at where she had got it from, not at Oliver Raden directly since his involvement would be assumed from the first, but at where he in turn had obtained the explosive. That meant time perhaps, but the result would be inevitable. Sheila Raden wasn't the type of girl you could call in and grill till she finally broke, but somewhere would be some little man, probably with a record too, and the police would break him as they broke most others. Whereupon they'd work backwards to Sheila Raden, whereupon even Russell could do little to help her. Sheila Raden was in the open now, and girls in the open, alone, were seldom dangerous.

But she wasn't alone, there was Oliver Raden. Kin frowned as he weighed it—it wasn't easy. The balance had swung against him there for the attempt on Raden had wretchedly failed. That could only mean that he'd had protection, which could only have come from a single source. Kin's frown became a steady scowl. . . . The Security Executive! That was ominous and maybe worse. He was too sophisticated to assume that Charles Russell had been given precise instructions by his Government since he knew that in the Executive's world a casual nod and four words unsaid were often more productive than two pages of careful orders marked *To Memorize and Destroy*. But the fact remained that the Executive had been interested, and it wasn't a body to act without motive. So what motive had it been given? It was exceedingly unlikely that the Government would dare back Sayed openly but a great deal less improbable that they had heard about the gold. They would know how things stood in Shahbaddin, and in any case two million in gold was a serious sum to allow to escape the country. The Government mightn't be bankrupt yet but it accounted its bullion frugally.

All this was bad for Mr Kin, by no means balanced by the knowledge that Oliver Raden was apparently holed up in Miss Raden's flat. That had been reported to him by the shadow whom he'd put on her, but he'd realized at once that it didn't eliminate Raden. He could ripen his plans in a woman's flat just as well as he could at the Ransome hotel, and though he'd been escorted there by what was certainly Russell's agent there wasn't any evidence that he was under the least restriction. He could leave one night quite freely when at last his plan was ready, and though Kin's own men could follow him it was certain he'd have protection again. Come to that he might have more than protection if Kin had guessed right about Russell's intentions; he might have active co-operation then, and from the Executive that would be final. Final, that is, unless Kin acted first and it was clear from his instructions that he must do so or face failure. But Raden was now of interest to the Security Executive, no less. A second move against such a man would be simple madness.

Which left only the third choice open, Geoffrey Addis. Kin considered him carefully for on the face of it he looked promising. If any man stranger to Raden blood had known of the gold and where it was old Addis would have been that man. He'd been Sir Montagu's friend and was Sheila's trustee, and though he was dead his son was his heir. His executor too for Kin had checked. Geoffrey Addis could well have knowledge now, and if he had could be made to yield it.

So this morning Kin walked to Mastertons with a quiet confidence he felt justified. Geoffrey Addis was vulnerable— vulnerable on two fronts. Sheila Raden had made a fool of him so he wouldn't be simply outraged and hurt at any suggestion which damaged her interests. In Kin's shrewd opinion he wasn't a man to forgive or forget, but if that were mistaken Kin had much more powerful levers to exploit the more serious weakness. For his competent organization had come up with the dirt he'd demanded, Clement Addis's debts, his wife's wild gambling, even the ten thousand cheque which had bounced at the Gardenia. That had been paid though God knew how: all He'd know was the soul of a brave old man now presumably damned for ever. Kin had it all or thought he had, and the one item he hadn't was shortly to be presented to him. To his total astonishment Geoffrey Addis was to tell him.

Kin went into Mastertons with a certain assurance; he held an excellent hand in a game he loved, extortion in its most interesting form, the pressure game *par excellence*. He saw that he'd been lucky too, for Geoffrey for once was behind the counter, talking to a dowager with a deference Kin found disgusting. An assistant came up and offered help but Kin shook his head politely. He'd wait for Mr Geoffrey please, and they brought him a chair to do it.

Presently the old woman left and Kin rose from his chair as she did so. He was certain that Geoffrey had noticed him but he wasn't by any means sure of a welcome. He could see Geoffrey hesitate and he hadn't come to Mastertons to suffer a resounding snub; he took three short steps forward and stood at the counter. Geoffrey was putting a tray away and as he turned Kin said quietly:

'I decided not to telephone.'

'And now that you've come here?' The manner was as chilly as a formal man could make it.

'I'd like a private word with you, one quite different from last time.'

'May I ask what about?'

'Let's say about your father's death.'

Geoffrey hesitated again, resentment competing with an evident curiosity. And was there something else in that English face? Kin thought there was and he hoped it was apprehension. So far so good, but he'd have to play his cards carefully. Well, he was very good at that. He liked the game, no, loved it.

Geoffrey was considering still and Kin believed he could read him. He didn't wish to talk to Kin but nor would he risk a scene in Mastertons. He turned on his heel at last, shrugging in irritation and something more.

'We'd better go into my office.'

They went into the little room and Geoffrey left Kin standing. 'Well?'

'Do you mind if I sit down?'

Geoffrey didn't answer but made a gesture which could mean anything. Mr Kin sat down deliberately and Geoffrey Addis followed him. Kin said conversationally:

'I believe we could co-operate.'

'Not that again.' Addis was emphatic.

'Not that again at all.'

'Then how could we co-operate?'

Kin told him in six short sentences, watching his face. Anger he could have coped with, incredulity persuaded. The one thing he feared was laughter.

But Geoffrey didn't laugh at him. His manner was still frigid but he was speaking with an interest which he wasn't trying to hide. A simple, unfrightened interest. Kin was puzzled.

'You really believe this gold exists?'

'It could and I'm told it does.'

'I see. And why should I help you get it?'

Kin answered that too, laying his hand down smoothly, watching Geoffrey Addis again. A safe had been blown at a reputable jewellers, a safe on which a High Commissioner held an injunction. The blowing had been effected by a charge contained in a briefcase, and the son of the house had put that briefcase in the safe. Never mind the legal niceties—the responsibility was unquestionable. Mastertons were responsible and Mastertons had a background which could hardly withstand a public scandal. There was, to start, a suicide, and eminent jewellers at the top of their trade very seldom shot their brains out for no better reason than that their firm had suffered a safe-blowing. But they might if their business were smothered in debt, if their private lives were crumbling, if much younger wives were compulsive gamblers at the Gardenia. In which case, or any part of it, an heir would be wise to co-operate.

Kin had watched Geoffrey closely as he laid down his cards in ascending order, but he'd barely got half-way through the hand when he realized that there was something wrong. Resentment he'd noticed and even anger. Both had been expected and he knew perfectly how to deal with them, but he'd expected fear too and there wasn't the least glimmer of it. Instead there was more than a casual hint of the only reaction which Kin really feared. Geoffrey hadn't yet laughed but he was smiling and it was genuine. Kin knew for he was experienced. Geoffrey Addis wasn't bluffing. He said calmly as Kin finished:

'That's a very neat piece of blackmail.'

'Let's call it a powerful hand instead.'

'It is.'

'And so?'

'So I'm calling it.'

'You can't.'

'I have.' Geoffrey Addis lit a cigarette, not offering one to Mr Kin. 'Let me tell you something else,' he said, 'something your, er, research work doesn't seem to have thrown up.' The amusement was overt now and Kin was anxious. 'The only good piece was a diamond tiara worth maybe fifty thousand. When the safe was blown it wasn't there. Am I boring you?'

Kin shook his head.

'The police traced it quite quickly and now hold it in their possession. You'd have heard that officially sooner or later but the police seem to be treading delicately—you guess why. So fifty thousand pounds' worth of stuff was not in the safe where it should have been, and only two people here knew the combination. I was one and I'm alive. The other was my father, and as you've just reminded me my father blew his brains out.'

'Why are you telling me this? It doesn't help you.'

'I hadn't quite finished. You know about my stepmother and you know about the Gardenia. So now I'll tell you something else. My father paid her debts there, which were ten thousand pounds, give a hundred either way. He paid by cheque. And the same day he drew it he paid in another, also for ten thousand pounds. And it came from another jeweller.'

'Why tell me this?' Kin asked again. He was very much more than anxious now, Mr Kin was plain uneasy.

'Because your hand's *too* bloody good—you can't blackmail me, I'm past it. My father's debts were much worse than you know and the business is a partnership. I'll have to sell a good deal of it and I'm negotiating already. Perhaps the new buyers would keep me on but I don't think I'd really want to stay.' Geoffrey looked at Kin indifferently. 'Mastertons,' he said, 'is finished—finished as an Addis firm. You're pushing at the empty air.'

'But the stolen tiara you've just told me about.' Kin knew that it wasn't much of a shot, but it was just, only just, worth firing.

'My father's dead, God damn you all. You can't touch my father.'

'And the ten thousand pounds he took for it?'

'Becomes one of his debts like any other. He sold it to a jeweller. Dog doesn't eat dog.'

Kin rose with a certain dignity. He knew when he'd failed and could accept defeat with decency.

Geoffrey Addis said sharply: 'Sit down.'

An astonished Mr Kin sat down. He was staring at Geoffrey Addis again and he wasn't much liking the man he saw. He was certainly a stranger to him, saying almost contemptuously:

'So we're agreed you can't blackmail me?'

Kin didn't answer, watching still.

'But I haven't yet said I wouldn't help you.'

'So you know where the gold is?'

'We'll come to that later.'

'But you'd help me?'

'On terms.   *My* terms.'

'Then lay them on the line,' Kin said.

'Not so fast. Aren't you interested in my motives?' Geoffrey was speaking with a patience which was insulting. 'If we're going to do business you ought to know my motives.'

'Yes, I suppose I should.' Kin was thinking that they were obvious. The man needed money and inevitably would ask for it. Kin was ready to make him promises.

'One of them's plain enough. I'd like to save Mastertons, live as I always have. But I also have a score to settle and I'd very much like to settle it. You understand what I mean? Would this gold go to the Radens if you don't get it? To Miss Raden in particular?'

. . . So the English had their own cool pride and it was dangerous to affront it. Kin had thought that before but the thought had been an abstraction. This soured and vindictive man was not. Kin caught his breath for suddenly he had cards again. He'd always believed he held them but he'd thought of them as a poor second best, hardly worth playing when straight blackmail was available. Straightforward commercial black-mail—it seldom failed. Today it had. Not that that mattered now at all. This new Geoffrey Addis was more vulnerable than ever.

He was asking again: 'You understand what I mean, whom I'm talking about and why?'

'And may I say I sympathize.'

Addis ignored this icily. 'Good. Then we'll take that side first.' He was the plenipotentiary dictating the terms of an unconditional surrender. 'You enter into an undertaking that you will not pursue Mastertons for negligence or for anything else. You can do as you wish about the civil case against the Radens.'

'Agreed—very easily. And the civil case doesn't interest me now. We can call it off and I will.'

'But there ought to be a criminal too and for some reason they're going slow on it. I want that righted and you can help. You've a High Commissioner behind you and I want all his weight thrown squarely in. There was a crime on these premises and I want to see it prosecuted. Perhaps I made a mistake myself and I'll admit it in court if I have to. But I wasn't a common criminal. I want the criminals caught and punished, one in particular. You follow me?'

'Perfectly.'

. . . My God, I underestimated. The man could be a Sicilian, not a nice one.

'Then we can come to the money. How much is this gold worth?'

'I'm told that it's worth two million pounds.' It had occured to Kin that he might say less, but the stupid lie was never worth while. If Addis did find the gold he'd know its value.

'Then a hundred thousand pounds would be five per cent.'

'It's a great deal of money.'

'Nonsense. I could press you much higher but I'm not acting solely for money.'

'I realize that.'

. . . Indeed I do and the smell offends me.

'But I do need some money and I'm asking for only that. My father's ordinary debts were sixty thousand, and to that you can add another ten to settle up for the tiara. And I owe it to his memory to provide for his widow decently.'

. . . And that's the sop to what's left of his conscience.

Kin asked again practically: 'Do you know where the gold is?'

'Frankly, no. But I've a very good idea.'

'When could you get to it?'

'By tomorrow or not at all.'

'Payment?'

'Cash when I find it and can tell you where it is. I'll take the High Commissioner's cheque, not yours.'

'Very well,' Kin said. There was nothing else he could. He rose and left with a stiff little bow. They didn't shake hands for neither man wished to.

Russell and George Willis were together again that evening and Russell was doing the listening. Willis was saying unhappily:

'So you see, we can't hold off Miss Raden much longer.'

'I didn't really expect you could.'

'We still realize what time may mean to you but it's getting a bit too hot to hold. No arrests and there ought to be. After all, the girl admitted that she handed in the briefcase, and though she lied about where she got it, it didn't take too much time to expose the lie. We checked on it.'

'And much else, I don't doubt.'

'It wasn't at all difficult. We know she knows Oliver Raden and we learnt from you that one of Raden's contacts is a craftsman and a good one. Naturally we've been talking to him.'

'You can prove the chain?'

'Not just yet in a court, but we've plenty to justify pulling two people in. One of those, I'm afraid, would be Sheila Raden. Then the least sort of break and it's Oliver too.'

'I can see your position perfectly.'

'And we're under more direct pressure too. A young ass has been round from the Commonwealth Relations Office. It took him twenty minutes to say what a human being would say in two, but the burden of the blah-blah was that the High Commissioner's hopping mad. He wants action and to see it.'

'Curious,' Charles Russell said. He was puzzled and Willis noticed it.

'Why curious?'

'Well, it wasn't his safe.'

'He was trying to get the contents and Mastertons let some Raden or Radens blow it under their noses. That's how he'd see it from what he must know. He knows about the tiara too —that it wasn't in the safe when it was blown. We had to tell him that this morning when our solicitor made his mind up that it'd be safer to let him in on it. "On balance," was what our lawyer said. They always say that in case they're wrong.'

'When was the High Commissioner told? Before this young idiot called from the C.R.O.?'

'Yes, sometime this morning.'

'Odder and odder. No gold was in that safe at all, and if the tiara, the only valuable piece, was in your hands . . ." Charles Russell frowned. 'Where's the motive for pressing you?'

'With every respect, sir, I believe that's a side issue. Or rather it is to me. I don't know His Excellency's motives, and from where I sit they hardly matter. What matters is that we're being pressed. Results. A prosecution or else. The big boys don't like it.'

'No more would I.'

'So you see how we stand. Your side's political, and I can perfectly see that anything affecting a Raden could be embarrassing to say the least. So I hate to withdraw a hand we freely offered but . . .' The Chief Super let the sentence float, looking at Charles Russell in an obvious embarrassment.

Russell didn't increase it but rose instead. 'I quite understand. . . . How long?'

'Till tomorrow at midday.'

'And then?'

'I'll have to pull Sheila Raden in. Then the slightest crack and Oliver too.'

'You'll be entirely right to do so.'

CHAPTER TEN

Mary Maguffy had left Sheila's duplex smiling, observing that the sofa was small, that the bed would hold more than one comfortably. If she'd happened to call next morning she'd have been gently disappointed but she'd have nodded understandingly at a situation she would have recognized. There was no profit in love with an unhappy man. It was barely worth taking your clothes off.

Sheila had known this also though she'd gone bitterly unsatisfied. She was a sincere and unshaken Moslem, but the Islam of Shahbaddin was a great many miles both in distance and in spirit from the fiercely protestant Islam of the barren desert lands which had given it birth. She had never gone heavily veiled in her life and only occasionally, and that on journeys, seen a wretched woman wearing one. Nor had she been instructed that she must nail her marriage lines to the bridal bedhead: that would have been an impertinence, a foolish human interference in something fore-ordained. Men and women were men and women as the Almighty had so made them, and though casual sex was entirely unthinkable, so was any view of it but an accepting, unfussy realism. But a woman was God's creature too, entitled to comport herself as in His wisdom he had created her, so if you desired a man sufficiently you welcomed him into your bed. But as a woman you didn't invite him, that wouldn't be seemly, might just conceivably be wicked. More important it wouldn't be fruitful, or not with a man as unhappy as Oliver. She had something to give still and wished it taken in the grand manner. It was better on all counts to await the auspicious moment. That was orthodox doctrine and no man could impeach it. Not even Oliver and he didn't seem to want to.

He was pacing the room that afternoon but at last sat down and smiled at her. It was a sad uncharacteristic thing. 'I've made a terrible mess of the job they gave me.'

'I don't see why.'

'It's kind of you to comfort me, but don't. I was sent here to get that gold. I haven't. I've got nowhere near it or even where it is. Instead I'm holed up here with you. I get myself attacked and a woman comes out of nowhere and saves my skin.'

'If you accept that the gold exists at all I think that attack was hopeful. It means somebody else must believe in it.'

He managed a slightly less ravaged smile. 'You don't?'

'Not really, even yet. We weren't that sort of people, you know.'

'I've got to assume it does exist or I might just as well creep home.'

'It was a cruel sort of job to send you on, as cruel in its different way as those Chinese who tortured you. "There's Raden gold in England," they said. "You're a Raden so go and get it."'

'You could look at it like that, I suppose. I can't.'

He spoke with an undertone of something close to disapproval and for a moment she was irritated. Didn't the man realize that she was utterly committed now? She was committed to his cause, which put in its simplest form was to prevent a minority from seizing power in their country, a minority which she'd been taught it was contemptible to hate but equally that it was madness to trust them further than you could see them. It had been an easy commitment to a cause she approved instinctively, but she knew very well that it wasn't the essential. It could have been bimetalism, the flat earth, something out of Mary Baker Eddy by Sigmund Freud on an off morning: she'd have followed Oliver Raden just as gladly. She sighed for he'd annoyed her, but she put her own frustration below this haggard man's unhappiness.

'Would it help if we talked?'

'Probably not but I'm ready to listen.'

She forgave him again at once. He hadn't meant to be

ungracious or even realized that he had been. He'd put himself on some private rack and she'd have to help.

'How much is this gold supposed to be?'

'When I left they were saying a million, now I hear it's nearly two.'

'That's an awful lot of gold.'

'It is. With that in our hands———'

'I know, you explained. What I meant is that it's an awful *lot*.'

He looked up quickly, as quickly interested. 'You're thinking something. Tell me.'

'It probably isn't useful, but what do you know about gold —the thing? What does two million look like? How big is it?'

For the first time he gave her his ordinary smile. 'You've been reading the Positivists. "How big is it? What does it feel like? What does it do?" '

'I don't know what you're talking about but I don't think the question was silly.'

'And nor do I.' He was serious again at once. 'I thought the gold might be in that safe and we took steps to find out that it wasn't. What you're really asking me is whether it ever could have been.'

'Yes, I suppose I am.'

'And where it could be now, given its size. Could it go in a normal safe or would it have to be a strongroom?'

'You put it much better than I could.'

'That's something to my credit then.' His irony was out again but she could see it was against himself, not her. 'You have a point, you have indeed.'

He'd been speaking with sudden energy but it left him just as suddenly. 'A pro would have thought of that before but I still ought to find it out.'

'Why don't you do that?'

'How can I?' He was miserable, deflated again. 'I've a friend who would know but I can't put him on further risk. I doubt if I'm quite a prisoner here but that delightful Mrs Maguffy said she'd be hanging around till they took her off. I don't suppose she'd stop me if I went out but I'm equally sure she'd follow. I can't risk that, not with things as they are. I'm useless and that hurts like hell.'

She didn't try to comfort him now, sensing he was beyond it; she asked instead practically: 'Couldn't you reach your friend through the Ransome?'

'I doubt it now, he'll be lying very low.'

'Very well,' she said, 'then *I'll* find out.'

'You could?' He was astonished.

'I've got a friend too, we spoke about him once. He's a solicitor called David Marks and he'd know or could discover.'

'But wouldn't he be suspicious if you asked him?'

'Very. But I think he'll keep his mouth shut.'

'Why?'

'That's my business,' she said coolly.

'You know him well?'

'No, hardly at all.'

'I don't like the idea of your involving yourself with men you hardly know.'

'You'll have to take that.'

She could see he was wickedly jealous and his jealousy didn't displease her. She thought with a prick of mischief that he had very good reason to be so. She was perfectly conscious of her effect on David Marks: he hadn't even tried to hide that what she did to him was send him. He was a randy young Jew but she wasn't the least race-conscious, and as for the adjective it was really only a compliment. Why not since God had made him so? David Marks was a man, and an evening in his company could be many things but not boring.

She went to the telephone and rang Lewis and Lee. She didn't fish since she knew she didn't need to—nothing about an unexpected evening free. She was a beauty and aware of it and said regally that she'd like to see David Marks. Who invited her to dinner on the fourth sentence they exchanged. . . . Tonight? But how fortunate—fortunate for David Marks. As she put back the receiver Oliver Raden said uneasily:

'I don't like this at all, you know.'

'I'd better go and titivate.'

She did so reflectively. David Marks would certainly help her, she hadn't the least doubt of it. She might have to pay a price perhaps, but she was perfectly ready to do so. A reasonable price and nothing more.

And she would decide the reason.

David Marks had hung up too. They were meeting at seven and it was now six o'clock. He rang an important client, cancelling their previous engagement for the evening. He then left his office and started walking to his club. On the way he bought a new silk shirt since he didn't keep spares at Lewis and Lee. He had himself carefully shaved and took a bath. When he had dressed he rubbed his hands. It was the gesture he had determined to break but this time he didn't check it. He had a right to rub his hands, he thought.

What a lay!

Within two minutes of arriving at the restaurant where David Marks took her Sheila could see that he was both respected and had the right to be. He had taken a good deal of trouble, but unlike Geoffrey Addis he had taken it first, by telephone. They sat down in the bar, agreeably plushy and scorning gimmicks of modern decor, and the *mâitre* presented her with an orchid. David Marks had ordered it. He had gentile friends who had hinted rather patronizingly that orchids could be thought a little vulgar, but none of them had persuaded him that orchids weren't also beautiful. So he bought his women orchids, and if they didn't appreciate orchids they could simply do the other thing. They wouldn't be worth the labour of further pursuit. With the flower was a tray of drinks, a glass of champagne for David and fresh lime juice for herself. Sheila looked at David gratefully. Real lime juice wasn't so easy to find and the bastard brew in bottles she detested. It had never even occurred to her that David Marks was a trifle brash: if she'd known the word she'd have thought of panache. She didn't but did not feel its loss. All she knew was that she was liking him. It was going to be an evening.

They were conducted to eat with a practised pomp, and to start with there was a hot hors d'oeuvre of *bouchées* filled with some fish she didn't recognize. David told her casually that the filling wasn't lobster or crab, and at once his stock moved a clear point higher. So he'd troubled to discover that she didn't eat shellfish. That was considerate but Geoffrey Addis might have done the same. This was true but he'd have bumbled it, telling her importantly, almost conspiratorially, too obviously seeking approval for his own quite simple foresight. David Marks, on the contrary, merely stated the fact, throwing the loaded line away with the confidence of a West End actor in drawing-room comedy. And she realized that he had order-ed for her. Good. She enjoyed her food but disliked its choosing.

With the lamb David Marks began to talk and for the third time she thought of Geoffrey Addis. Geoffrey talked well but only up to a certain point. Take him beyond it and he'd simply stare, clam up. But David began where Geoffrey finished, not talking for effect but with a natural and unforced bubble. He was sticking to the champagne but she'd changed to un-iced water. It had been brought without her having to ask. There was the minimum chat with the waiters—she liked that too. David Marks was asking her:

'Have you ever been to a Bunny Club?'

'No, but I know what they are. But if you were thinking of taking me——'

'Good God, no, they make me sick.' He was suddenly and genuinely indignant. 'I've nothing against old uncle sex, I'm a male and delighted to be one. What turns me up is an organized tease, and when it's commercial too it's plain disgusting. Those terrible tired businessmen, forty-ish but senescent. Can you imagine a Frenchman in a Bunny Club? The civilization where they thrive deserves the bomb on it tomorrow. I'd rather see a daughter in a brothel.'

'I know what you mean. If it came to the point I think I'd rather work in one myself. At least it would be honest.'

He'd moved up another notch on her private score. He was

telling her what he was after and she respected him for wanting to; he was also doing it with some delicacy and she liked her men intelligent. It was going to be an evening, yes indeed.

'Tell me why you're eating with me. I'm a Jew and hardly your class.' From nine men in ten the question would have made her squirm but David could ask it simply and leave her laughing.

'I thought I'd enjoy your company and I wanted to ask a question.'

'Ask it.'

'What do you know about gold?

He looked at her sharply. 'There was a safe blown at Mastertons and the full story isn't out yet. The circumstances were odd, though.' He drank some champagne. 'Suspicious if you'll accept the word.'

'Why shouldn't I accept it?'

He smiled but didn't answer, asking another question instead. 'I've heard about the tiara, by the way. It wasn't in your safe when the safe got done. All very odd but not yet formally my business. I hope it never will be.' His sharp look was now the shrewdest stare. 'Are you talking to your solicitor?'

'No.'

'Then I'm not talking to a client. So going back to the gold again, what do you want to know?'

'How does it come? How big is it?'

'How big is how much?'

'Say two million pounds.'

He whistled but didn't query it. 'Too big to have been in that safe,' he said.

'You're sure?'

'Pretty sure. I'll find out for certain if that's what you want, but there's a mystique about gold in the City of London. If I rang up a bullion-man he'd want to know why I was asking, and if I didn't tell him he'd probably make a note and inform the police. Nonsensical but that's how it goes. But I'm perfectly certain two million's a great deal physically.' He reflected, unconsciously dropping his voice. 'It comes in all shapes and sizes. There are the little blocks you smuggle out in a specially constructed waistcoat, and there's a smaller than normal but legal size which they use when they want to send by air. But there's something like a standard bar too, though it isn't rigidly standardized. Given normal assay it's worth something over five thousand pounds, or five or six times that if you can get it, say, to India.'

'How big are they?'

'I've only seen them twice in my life and I didn't indulge in measuring. If I had to guess I'd say eight or ten inches by four or five. About that. Often they slope to the top—that is, it's narrower than the bottom. Or perhaps I should be saying that the ones I once saw did.'

'And you say they're worth five thousand each?' She did some simple mental arithmetic. 'So two million pounds would be four hundred bars.'

He laughed. 'I make the sum the same.'

'And they're ten by four or thereabouts?'

'I guessed at that, I didn't state.'

'I don't think I'll work the size out—I don't think I need to. Even if you're rather wrong, even if it were only one million, it'd still be far too big.'

He asked softly: 'Too big for what?'

'Too big for me.'

He opened his mouth but shut it quickly; he looked at her again, then smiled and shrugged. 'There's a soufflé,' he said. 'I hope you like soufflés.'

'Oh yes, I like soufflés.'

And David Marks, she was thinking, too. If it hadn't been for Oliver she could have considered him quite seriously. Not a gentleman perhaps—a man. It was what she wanted. The waiter brought coffee but David declined the brandy. Sensibly, Sheila Raden thought, since he clearly intended venery. He was giving her the frankest stare but she wasn't at all put out by it. Geoffrey Addis, off guard, had chanced the same sort of look but there'd been a subtle, offensive difference: he had looked at her with a pair of eyes but their two messages hadn't been quite the same. One had said impersonally that this attractive girl had money too, the other that she was beautiful, that she wouldn't be intolerable in the bed of a man of taste. But David's frank stare was much more honest: he'd have to lay her and lay her quick or he wouldn't sleep a wink that night. A pity that, but he'd know the cure and it wouldn't be in a Bunny Club.

David dealt with the bill unfussily but checking it carefully first; he then left a generous tip and signed. As he held the taxi's door for her he said:

'Come back to my flat and I'll brew some more coffee.'

'I'd like to but I'm short of sleep.'

'Just as you say.' He was far from despairing since he knew she lived alone.

In the taxi he started making love and she accepted it composedly. She knew that he lit no spark in her but also that a week ago he might very well have done so. So she returned his kisses graciously, even warmly. He took another minor liberty and for a second Sheila hesitated. But he was still within the canon and if doing it gave him pleasure. . . .

He then took a major liberty and she gasped. It was Moira Perry again but alarmingly more adroit. For a second she was frightened, not with a panic fear of assault or worse, but for herself, for the man's experience and scaring skill.

It had been a very good dinner but not that good.

She reacted at once and David yelped. He let go of her quickly, sliding away on the taxi's seat. Back in his own corner he said crossly:

'My God, I thought you'd done me.' He was rubbing his person ruefully.

'I could if I'd wanted to.' She was perfectly cool: it was a statement of fact.

'Where did you learn that one?'

'At school.'

'But I thought you were at a convent.'

'I was.'

'Some convent.'

'Don't get it wrong. That wasn't part of what the Reverend Mother taught us. I learnt it from the other girls.'

'Some girls.'

'Oh, I don't know. Shahbaddin was a funny place. Nine-tenths of the time it was safer than Knightsbridge.' They were then in Exhibition Road. 'But the odd time out you had to know how to take care of yourself.'

'You're very slick at it,' he said.

'It isn't at all difficult. You keep one nail a little longer than the others——'

'Don't tell me please—I'd rather not know.' His good humour was returning for he'd always been able to laugh against himself. 'Tell me,' he said, as the worst of the pain eased, 'have you done that before?'

'I've practised it.'

'With the other girls? I should have thought that with other girls there would be certain technical difficulties.'

'No, we used squash balls.'

He began to laugh on his normal note but with a hint of sharp embarrassment behind. 'And now you'll expect an apology.'

'Why should I?' Her surprise was wholly genuine, he could see she wasn't acting.

'Well. . . .'

'I'm annoyed of course, but I'm not really angry.' She looked at him reflectively. He was a male and she liked him. It simply wasn't seemly to humiliate a decent man. 'The fact is,' she said, 'I've a man of my own.'

'I'm sorry, I didn't know.'

'It's a pity in its way. If I hadn't——'

'That doesn't help me at all but it's nice of you to tell me.'

Back at the duplex he handed her out, saying with simple dignity: 'We shan't meet again, or not outside the office.'

'I understand that. And would you misunderstand me if I said that in a way I'm glad?'

'I'll take that the way I hope you mean it.'

'Do that.' She kissed him unexpectedly and was gone.

He watched her run up the steps, then went back to the taxi. The driver was grinning rudely. 'Bad luck, guv,' he said. 'I gotta mirror.'

'Shut your face or I'll do the same for you.' David gave him an address in North West Three. It was an admirable arrangement, and David, tonight, had never been more grateful for its existence. Some unsuspecting goy paid the lady's rent and David was always welcome there. He said to the driver crisply: 'And get there fast.'

CHAPTER ELEVEN

Sheila Raden went up in the lift and let herself in. She opened the door quietly, conscious that she bore news which must be unwelcome. Oliver had been sitting but rose as she came in. He walked across to meet her but he walked without spring, like a man in a sickness. 'What news?' he asked.

His tone dropped her spirit like lead on stone. 'What news?' —you should ask it eagerly. But Oliver sounded resigned at best, and a stoic resignation was a mood she'd never seen him in. Nor did she like it, this wasn't her man. 'He told me what I asked,' she said.

'The gold?'

'Two million pounds would be four hundred bars and their size is around ten inches by four.'

'So it couldn't have been in the Mastertons' safe?'

'I'm sure of that now.'

'Is there another safe at Averley?'

'A tiny thing in the study wall. For money and papers, nothing more.'

'We're finished,' he said dully. 'Finished and helpless. The gold must be in some strongroom at a bank. Very likely it isn't gold by now but money in some damned account. There'll be somebody who can instruct on it but that somebody isn't me or even you.'

The words came out flatly but with anger chasing their laggard heels. That was promising, she thought: an honest rage might relieve his bitter tension. Sheila said deliberately: 'Would that be too bad? If the money's tied up then we can't reach it. But no more can our enemies.'

He almost lost his temper and she heartily hoped he was going to. 'I've got to have that money. I must.'

'But why?' It was an infuriating question and she meant it to infuriate. He was slowly coming alive again.

'I've told you a dozen times. If Sayed had that gold or better the money——'

She shook her head. 'But the last news you had from your friends was good. You told me that too. There'll be a crisis in Shahbaddin in a week at most and if Sayed's the man you think he is the money can't matter that much now. If I'd brought you the gold in a lorry tonight, what then? You couldn't have sent it to Sayed in time.'

He looked at her with an expression coming close to plain resentment. 'What are you trying to do to me?'

'I'm trying to make you think,' she said.

'I think about that gold all the time. I'm mewed up here all day, a failure——'

'That's what I meant. You're not a failure.'

He sat down on the sofa, patting the vacant place. She ignored the gesture totally, it invited what she didn't want; she pulled up another chair and faced him. 'You think you're a failure,' she said again. 'You're not.'

'I haven't got that gold and I never shall.'

'It was a damfool errand. No clues to the whereabouts and only rumours about the amount.'

'Perhaps—I won't dispute it now. But somehow I've got to prove to myself that I'm any sort of a man at all.'

With the last of a woman's patience she said: 'I don't see why you should ever doubt it. I don't. They tortured you, didn't they? You took it and lived.' He had temporarily taken his gloves off and his hands tore her heart when she made herself look at them.

'But I screamed and screamed. Then the others came and rescued me. What did I do to help myself?'

It was Sheila now who lost her temper. 'Oh God,' she said, 'you're a terrible fool.'

He gave her his sudden crooked smile, half of irony, half of the need she knew they shared. It had never failed to ravish her and now it was unbearable. 'You know why I've got to prove myself.'

'I can guess and you're very wrong.'

'But that's how I feel, I can't escape it.' He was speaking so softly she could hardly make the words out, softly but he was stubborn still.

'I'm concerned in this too.' She leant forward and touched the sofa. 'This isn't a comfortable place to sleep.' It was the nearest she'd ever bring herself to inviting him to take her.

'No, I don't sleep well but that isn't the reason. I'll just have to manage.'

She rose with a sigh, defeated and aware of it. 'In that case I'll have a bath. And you?'

'I think I'll get drunk.'

She wasn't entirely horrified since she knew that he wasn't as strict as herself. He drank very seldom but just occasionally he would use the thing. That was for his own conscience, not for hers. She brought the whisky and a tumbler.

'May it do you good. And try not to snore.'

She ran a very hot bath and relaxed in it slowly, inspecting her body dispassionately as she lay supine, almost asleep. It really wasn't bad at all and that wasn't a woman's vanity. Her father in his army days had been a boxer of some competence and she had the boxer's wide and well-spaced chest. Naturally with a difference and she knew it was an important one. Men certainly seemed to find it so—she had recent and practical proof if she'd ever doubted. Her hips weren't big, but the tiny waist from which they flowered was the base for two proud and female curves. As for what she couldn't see, it would drive a Turk demented. She wasn't unlike that Goya nude, the one they told you was some drear duchess. Except, no doubt, that she'd be very much cleaner. A virgin too, and she didn't wish it.

Men were idiots with absurd ideas. Not David Marks, he was splendidly uncomplicated. He'd have taken her attritively, she'd have remembered it for a fortnight. Not that she would have resented that, it was in the book and therefore to be accepted. But she simply hadn't wanted him now. What she wanted was fourteen feet away, drinking himself into an animal stupor. For no reason at all but some ridiculous self-doubt.

Men. . . .

The cooling water woke her and she dried herself unhappily. 'Men,' she said aloud but softly. 'Men, men, men.' They were impossible to understand but you didn't amount to much if you didn't have one.

As David Marks's taxi dropped him in one of the more modest streets of St John's Wood another drove out of it. He paid it no attention since he hadn't any reason to, but he would have been interested in its occupant. It was very rare indeed for Kin to risk personal contact with any member of the organization which had been put at his disposal, but tonight was quite exceptional, the most urgent of his life both for the matter he had at stake and for the very short time he had to work in.

The man he had been talking to owned a prosperous Chinese restaurant, and in his taxi Kin smiled. He thought the English quite extraordinary, not for their stupidity—that could be overestimated—but for their public, unstated fetishes. They weren't so stupid as to suppose that a Chinese with a Hong Kong passport wasn't still a Chinese by race and culture, and a man like Charles Russell would be alert to the fact and worried by it. Her Majesty's Chinese subjects could be losing him his beauty sleep, the ones who traded in his country, ran restaurants almost everywhere and could move about as freely as the citizens they lived with. Very probably he had broken it down: say sixty per cent who were passionately anti-communist, thirty per cent indifferent or sitting quietly on the historical fence, and ten per cent secretly dedicated to the same doctrine which drove Kin himself. The Executive would have a working list, and in that case the name of Kin's host that night would be very high indeed on it. So in any other country he'd have been quietly lost, deported. But not in England. Kin laughed aloud. The rule of law? It was partly that, but the Executive wasn't notorious for excessive genuflections at the shrine of the rule of law. No. But there was a decaying office in

Whitehall, an office staffed where it mattered by Foreign Office failures, men whose careers, their hope of honours, even their salaries, could collapse in a night if a phrase, a mystique, were unclothed as the sham it was. Kin found it mildly ludicrous and had British friends who found it worse. The phrase, the mystique, was the British Commonwealth.

It was ludicrous but convenient too. A few white sympathizers, few but entirely trustworthy, and a steady pool of dedicated and ruthless men. It was in no way extraordinary that their organization was an effective one.

Kin had taken a risk in calling in person but he'd considered and accepted it. Now he was sure that the risk had been worth while. He'd explained and the other Chinese had nodded. 'Yes,' he'd said simply, 'there isn't much time. If Sayed can strike at all he'll do it soon. With or without this gold.'

'But we're still under orders to get it. I've got a line on it at last but not directly.'

'How?'

'There's a young man called Geoffrey Addis and I can tell you where to find him. For reasons of his own he's prepared to help.'

The other Chinese smiled. 'I wasn't asking.'

'Perfectly correctly. But one of his terms is a hundred thousand pounds.'

'That's quite a lot of money and you know how we have to earn it.'

'He could have asked for four times that and I'd still have agreed. What's the difference when we're not paying him?'

'Like that?' the other said.

'Like that.'

'Then what do I do?'

'I'll give you his address and a photograph too. That's all you'll need with things as they are. He promised it by tomorrow or not at all. So he's got to act tonight.'

'And if he does lead me on to it?'

'I hope it'll be too much to move alone. So stay with it but ring me. I'll have transport standing by.'

'And this Geoffrey Addis?'
'You're to deal with Geoffrey Addis.'
'Dealing with meaning kill if I have to?'
'Dealing with meaning dealing with.'

A third car was moving that night and fast. It was Geoffrey Addis's Jaguar. He had put in the boot what he thought necessary for his purpose, buying the pitchfork and spade at an ordinary ironmonger since he didn't wish to take them from the comfortable house in Wimbledon. But he needed something to probe with too and that had been more difficult: it had to be two feet long at least and it must also be sharp and fairly strong. He had finally found what he wanted in a shop selling armour and ancient weapons, a formidable ridged French bayonet from the time of the First World War. All these were now with him as he drove down to Averley. He was something short of certain that he'd find gold at the Raden manor, but he'd told Kin the literal truth about his chances. He believed them to be better than good and had a very fair reason for thinking so.

He smiled sourly as he drove fast and well, thinking of Sheila Raden. She'd never talked to him very freely (she wouldn't, he'd decided now, since she'd ensnared him only to use him) but just occasionally she'd unbuttoned and he'd remembered a moment she'd done so. He had often tried to draw her out about Shahbaddin and her life there. As often she had slipped him, but once she'd been almost relaxed and gay and had casually told him a story. It really had been a folk tale, a fable about the Money Tree. That was in fact the magnolia, and it was widely believed the tree brought good fortune. It brought prosperity in general but in particular it bore that fine thing gold, and the sensible man who planted one buried gold amongst its seedling roots. It was a custom surviving from pagan days but there was still a strong pagan tradition in Shahbaddin. So it was decent and gracious to nourish a new magnolia, to feed it from its uncertain start on what you hoped it would finally yield you.

135

And there was a fine magnolia tree at Averley—Geoffrey had seen it. That could mean nothing at all but he'd guessed it might. At the worst it was a hunch worth playing. Geoffrey hadn't much sense of humour but could recognize it in others. The Radens—impossible people. It would be exactly the Raden idea of a joke to bury two million pounds in gold by a tree with a golden fable.

The Radens. . . . He scowled. A worthless lot, adventurers really, and the girl had been much worse than that. She'd humiliated and ruthlessly used him. He'd agreed to help Kin for a hundred thousand pounds he sorely needed, and it had been pleasant to reverse the cards against a bullying too-confident blackmailer, to make his own terms and to see them accepted. These had weighed but not decisively: what had made him say yes had been much more potent, the driving need to retaliate, somehow to soothe his savaged self-respect. He'd had time to think it over too and had realized that the gold was his sole real weapon. . . . The High Commissioner would press for a prosecution against Miss Raden? It was true that Kin had agreed to that but Geoffrey had begun to doubt if very much would come of it. Sheila would have good lawyers who might conceivably prise her off her hook, and even if they didn't it would still be a first offence. Perhaps not even jail at all, and nothing she couldn't take and come out the same. *And that simply wasn't good enough.* He'd had time to think but had used it instead to brood alone; a forgivable human desire to square a score had bitterly festered. An older man, any man with a sense of humour, would have recognized the symptoms and firmly warned him. Geoffrey had more than a suspicion that if he led Mr Kin to the gold he'd be somehow serving the interests of a state which wasn't his own; he had considered that but did not care. Sheila Raden wouldn't get it and that was that. It was his only effective tool and he meant to use it. As he drove down to Averley fast and well his coldly handsome face was blurred with hating. Mr Kin had been right and Sheila too. There was a second Geoffrey Addis and he wasn't an attractive one.

He didn't consider his mission dangerous as he drove past Averley's single and modest lodge. What risks did he run? He had convinced himself he ran none. It wasn't as though he could be caught transporting gold which he'd have to account for: all he need do was find it and tell Kin. Nevertheless he had armed himself. He was a jeweller in a respectable business and was sometimes obliged to take jewellery home, so it hadn't been very difficult to get a perfectly legal licence to keep a gun. Still, he had hesitated before he'd slipped it into a pocket. He hadn't fired a firearm since his days as a national serviceman, but a gun was a moral ally, a wicked forty-five which matched his mood.

He went past the lodge which he knew housed a gamekeeper, then right into a little lane. He knew where he was, for though he hadn't shot here himself he'd sometimes carried his father's second gun. A little further up the lane was what the Radens called the cottage, in fact the only comfortable part of Averley. The big house itself was the bleakest of barracks, not all of it furnished and what there was sparsely. It gave minimal comfort to men who were content to shoot till dark, then take a few drinks and an evening meal before they slept to recharge their energies. Geoffrey Addis didn't know if Sheila had let the shooting yet, but nor was he much worried that she might have. It was October the tenth and the pheasants would be legal game, but shooting at Averley never started before the twentieth. The house would be empty but the woods might not be. A conscientious gamekeeper was his only enemy.

He'd been running without lights since he'd turned into the unmetalled lane, for he knew the general layout and the moon was riding high. There was a lay-by near a wooden gate and Geoffrey eased the Jaguar in. He got out but returned at once. The car had been warm, a private world, and he'd forgotten how cold an October night in Hampshire could often be. He put on a heavy sweater and started again, taking the pitchfork, the spade and the old French bayonet. He put them carefully over the gate, picking them up when he followed himself. Any noise would be fatal, but he didn't intend to push his way through a wood which he didn't know too well. There was a track and he meant to use it. It led through the wood into open parkland, then perhaps half a mile of clear walking on grass to the splendid neglected garden. There was a parterre at its southern end and the Money Tree dreamed over it in the autumn moon's virgin nimbus.

Now he was through the wood without mishap, no roosting bird rising in noisy protest, no nightwalking keeper challenging his presence. He'd been carrying his implements at the Rifleman's long trail, but now he shouldered them confidently, marching across the parkland towards the garden. An ancient iron fence enclosed it groggily, but it was no sort of obstacle and he was over it in a second. He walked carefully through the ruin of what had once been an opulent border, out on to the parterre and the single majestic tree. There were some charming *amorini* but his eyes were for the tree alone. He had the impression that it was watching him—watching him and something more. He wasn't an imaginative man and he suppressed the thought with a shocked distaste.

He went to the tree and began to probe, working outwards from its base in widening circles. One circle, then two and three. . . . Nothing at all. Despite the cold small hours he'd started to sweat. He began on a fourth circle.

The bayonet stuck.

He was triumphant but puzzled. It hadn't the right feel, he thought—not of metal either naked or in a box. But it wasn't a stone for a stone wouldn't give. This had a certain spongy feel, almost a resilience. He probed again deliberately, making an outline pattern of the incisions; he stepped back and looked.

. . . Ten inches by four, a bar of gold in protective cloth, the first of the Radens' illegal hoard.

Geoffrey started to dig furiously, first with the pitchfork, then the spade. It took him longer than he'd expected but at last he could see a bundle. He freed it gingerly and picked it up—mouldering sackcloth, damp and heavy, almost completely decayed. The sackcloth was falling to pieces and for a moment he thought of the grave of some favourite dog. But the acutest of his senses reassured him. His heart racing he shook it gently and the outer rags fell away. The inner had more resistance still but when he pulled at them they began to shred.

A voice said softly: 'Give that to me.'

Geoffrey straightened at once, still holding the bundle. His first thought had been of gamekeepers, but a gamekeeper wouldn't be wearing a stocking mask. He asked stupidly and knowing it:

'Who are you?'

The other didn't answer him; he held out his hand, still silent.

Geoffrey Addis thought quickly. Under the stocking the face was a featureless blur, but there was something about the man, the shoulders, a stockiness, the way he stood. . . . He wasn't a European. Geoffrey looked at his hands but in the moonlight they were colourless.

The man uttered again sharply: 'Hand that over.' The speech had a clipped cadence impossible to mistake.

. . . A Chinese. So Kin was double-crossing him.

The Chinese was moving forward now, shuffling like a wrestler, his hands at the ready. He was squat but very powerful; he could take Geoffrey Addis and evidently meant to.

Geoffrey was frightened, steadily losing the struggle against an increasing and sickening panic. He couldn't cope with this man, he hadn't a chance; he could be beaten up mercilessly, maybe worse. He'd be found in a Hampshire garden dead. . . .

He pulled his gun, calling 'Stop' but the other didn't. He didn't even look at the gun but came on in a silent menace.

Geoffrey fired once. A single shot was all he had time for.

He knew from the first blow he'd missed—it wasn't the blow of a wounded man. It came with the side of the hand and it knocked the pistol spinning. It also broke Geoffrey's wrist though it made no difference. He was utterly outclassed.

The Chinese began to punish him. He was tempted to kill, he resented being shot at, but killing ran additional risks and he hadn't been told in terms he must. But he could dislocate and rupture and he did so methodically. At the end he was holding

Geoffrey up. He let him fall finally and picked up the bundle. He vanished into the darkness just as silently as he'd emerged.

The gamekeeper he'd been worried about found Geoffrey Addis in the first of the dawn, and forty minutes later he was in bed in the local hospital. The doctor would say that he'd live but nothing more.

At much the same moment Kin was listening to his agent's report. It had been factual and clear and Kin hadn't needed to put questions. On the table between them was a bundle of decaying rags. Kin was asking the other briefly:

'Is this all?'

'I can't be certain. I came back when I was sure our little scuffle had gone unnoticed, and I poked about with Addis's tools. I used gloves, of course.'

'You found nothing?'

'And proved nothing. About twenty-two inches was my limit with his probe. I didn't have time for digging at large.'

'And you haven't opened this?' Kin was nodding at the bundle.

The second Chinese said dryly: 'That pleasure I kept for you.'

'Very well.' Kin began on the bundle delicately, stripping off the layers one by one. As he went deeper the cloth became dryer. So did the bundle decrease in size. When it was almost finished Kin said:

'If this is gold it can't be a lot.'

'A marker perhaps?'

'Perhaps.'

Kin pulled off the last two layers and there was a folded linen handkerchief, almost unsoiled. In one corner was a monogram R. Kin handed it to the other Chinese.

'You did the work. You open.'

But the other man never did so. As Kin handed across the handkerchief something fell out of it onto the floor. Kin picked it up and held it out.

It was a single golden sovereign, mint new.

CHAPTER TWELVE

When the man who kept a restaurant had left Mr Kin sat down to think. He had been born in Shahbaddin which the other hadn't, and he knew the fable of the Money Tree. As also, it seemed, had Geoffrey Addis, and it had put him into hospital. He'd deserved it of course—pulling firearms was a dangerous ploy and a great deal worse than dangerous when you didn't know how to use them. Kin had gathered he'd be unconscious still, but he wouldn't die so he'd recover and talk. And then? He wouldn't have known his assailant but might have recognized his race. And then again? There were thousands of Hong Kong Chinese in the land and this one was a well-trained man. It was very long odds that the police would never trace him, but if by some chance they did one thing was sure. He'd never lead them to Mr Kin. This was England, they couldn't make him. God Save the Queen.

Kin dismissed Geoffrey Addis since he'd decided he'd nothing to fear from him and he had more important matters for his reflection. The first was the news from Shahbaddin. It depressed Mr Kin intensely. Sayed was technically still underground but no longer in semi-hiding. He was in fact in the capital now, not stumping the streets with gangs of armed men (he wouldn't, Kin thought, since he wasn't that kind) but with a bodyguard more than adequate to make a quiet liquidation impossible. So there'd been a stormy Cabinet meeting and the Chinese members had forced the issue. The man was a danger, he must be arrested or they'd resign *en bloc*. They had known that a tired and nervous junta would never face that, even the few not secretly committed to them, so a warrant had gone out for Sayed's arrest. That had been thirty-six hours ago and the warrant was still unexecuted. Mr Kin knew what that meant. It meant that the police were uncertain at best, that in any real disturbances they would quietly look the other way.

So now the gold hardly mattered? But it mattered to Kin desperately. Kin had his orders and they would stand until they were cancelled. He doubted they ever would be, or not till too late to disimpale him. He'd been becoming a little sceptical about that gold. Was there really two million and did it in fact exist at all? He sighed unhappily for his personal doubts were irrelevant. His orders remained and he remembered them grimly. . . . If he wanted it in concrete terms it must be put like this and in no other way: to obtain the gold would be straight success and successes were never forgotten, but if that were impossible then at least it must be neutralized. If Kin's masters couldn't have it then nor must Sayed. That wouldn't be success but nor would it be accounted total failure. Which likewise was never forgotten.

These orders stood and in a silence which Kin thought ominous. For several days there'd been a stream of them, then they'd stopped on the last one suddenly. Kin didn't like that since he was wholly without illusions. He had at his disposal an organization which he guessed lost Charles Russell some sleep at night, but though he could give it instructions he didn't control it. If he failed or was even thought to have failed other orders could go out to it, and that wouldn't be healthy for Mr Kin.

So he was inescapably back on the second best though he'd privately hoped he needn't be, trying to neutralize gold which he no longer quite believed in. Which meant neutralizing Oliver Raden. He couldn't escape it.

He concentrated, frowning. . . . But Oliver Raden was already neutralized, holed up in Sheila Raden's flat with a woman from the Executive marking him? Yes, but marking him for what—just for protection? Kin shook his head for he had considered this once before. The Executive might be co-operating and that would be conclusive if the gold did really exist. It was an if and he thought it a big one now, but he simply couldn't accept the risk, not accept the risk and look forward to ripe old age.

But nor could he act against Oliver Raden—he'd been forced to that decision too. That seemed to be weeks not days ago, at a time when he'd had the option to make his choices . . . Sheila Raden or Oliver, Geoffrey Addis. . . . Now he had no choice at all, only the pressing need to form a plan. A plan to stop Oliver Raden, who had an operator from the Executive camping on his doorstep and if and when he acted would be covered or even helped. Sheila Raden or Oliver, Geoffrey Addis. . . . Geoffrey had failed and no longer counted; Oliver was protected; Sheila Raden had powerful contacts and couldn't be touched. He'd written her off. . . .

But much too lightly.

It came to him suddenly, an echo from dull lectures which had bored him. He knew now that they shouldn't, that he'd been remiss, even wicked, in not thinking from first principles. It was Oliver he had to fear but he'd reach at him through Sheila. Sheila hadn't been arrested yet, Sheila was a Raden but so was her cousin Oliver. It was good strong blood still, it wouldn't shirk. They'd been capitalist exploiters but they hadn't become degenerates. Kin thought of the dull lectures again, smiling at last contentedly. He was remembering the words, the wagging forefinger, even the heavy Czech face.

You always got them through their women.

Charles Russell was in his office next morning at his usual time, which by Whitehall standards was the unheard-of hour of a quarter to nine. But he liked to get in early and always had. For one thing he woke at seven and could seldom sleep much after it, and for another he found it valuable to have an hour to think quietly before the telephone started its daily Stations of the Cross. And if, after lunch, he took half an hour in his leather chair, very well, he had earned it.

He was in excellent humour, humming a phrase from the opera he'd been to the night before. His taste in opera was uncomplicated and robust; he had no time for people who talked opera all day but seemed to find it shameful to accept a simple pleasure simply. Those tedious affairs in East Anglia, that strangulated lieder-singer pretending to be a tenor! Why, in Italy they wouldn't have let him on the stage. And as for Mozart in Sussex, you could have all of Sussex and much of Mozart. Charles Russell liked good red meat and the closer the bone the better. *Der Rosenkavalier*—now that was something. He'd been wallowing (his own word) the night before. Bloody marvellous. The Marschallin had lost her young lover and was taking it gracefully as the woman of the world she was, so the three of them stood there and sang it out, no tiresome action, just a glorious noise. *Hab' mir's gelobt*, the knife in the heart as the warm soprano went up and up, then you thought that the orchestra was coda-ing out, and Jesus it wasn't, the woman had five notes left. You couldn't take them but you had to, and back you came for more agony, time and time again. Now that was opera, the real thing. Unbearable.

Russell had been humming the superlative dying fall when the telephone interrupted him. He frowned for it was early still but he dutifully picked the receiver up. It was Chief Superintendent Willis and he killed Charles Russell's euphoria dead. Geoffrey Addis, the one from Mastertons, had been found on the Raden estate in Hampshire; he'd been brutally beaten up, was still unconscious but he'd live. Why had he gone there? Apparently to look for something. He'd had digging tools and had dug a hole, but nothing had been found in it, nor on Addis, nor in his abandoned car. What had been found was a pistol, and the local police had already checked that it was legally licensed to Addis. One shot had been fired and the only finger-prints were Addis's. This would be police work, at least at first, but in view of Russell's interest in the Radens and the Addises too Willis was reporting as a part of the good colleagues' net.

Russell thanked him and rang off. It would have been interesting to speculate, but Addis wasn't his major problem. That remained political but it was useless to ring his Minister. Russell well knew what Tuke would say. Harry Tuke would now know, as Russell did too, that Sayed in Shahbaddin had a very fair chance, and Sayed's success would suit Tuke and the

Cabinet perfectly. It would be what they'd all been hoping for, a strong but indigenous Government which could stand up to the Chinese. The last thing Harry Tuke would want would be a scandal here in England, a journalists' benefit about gold and the Raden family, attempts by a previous Government to secure it if it existed, an unexplained safeblowing, and finally personal violence which a competent reporter might well link with the men who'd planned it. None of this would be an auspicious start with a new Government you wished well to and hoped would last. So Tuke would beg Russell to take some action, do something, anything, get the Radens out of the country, for instance. . . .

He considered it quite seriously, for the idea was both tempting and perfectly possible. But finally he shook his head. It would by no means be difficult. On an airfield not far from London was a twin-engined aircraft at twenty minutes' notice and in a villa in the Appennines Russell had very good friends. So it wouldn't be difficult but it would be a shameless double-cross against friends he valued. The police had been wholly scrupulous, warning him that they'd pull Sheila in by twelve o'clock that morning. Almost certainly Oliver Raden to follow. So Russell snatches them both with minutes to go and the police think what? Charles Russell shuddered. He had a native distaste for double-crossing his friends but he was also a realist, a solid administrator, and when it came to a choice between a Minister and the police he couldn't hesitate. Chief Superintendent Willis was a much more valuable contact than Harry Tuke. Harry Tuke was a Cabinet Minister but a senior policeman could help you and often did.

He shook his head but rang down to Communications. 'Get me Mrs Maguffy, please.' He settled to wait for he knew the drill. She'd have a radio now but wouldn't use it in public: when her handbag began to click at her she'd kill the noise, then find somewhere to talk. When she came through he asked her at once:

'Where are you, please?'

'In a supermarket in Fulham Road.'

'Not using that thing in public, of course.'

'Of course not, I'm in the john.' A chuckle. 'On the door here it says Powder Room.'

'Raden's in the supermarket?'

'No, he's safely in the flat still. He hasn't left it since I took him there and they always keep the door closed. But the girl has to feed him so she goes out to do the shopping. I thought I could do worse than watch her.'

'You don't think it's a blind to draw you off?'

'It could be—I'd bet against it.'

'Then listen, I've got news for you.' He told her what Willis had just passed on. The radio whistled and Russell asked: 'Any theories on that?'

'It doesn't make much sense to me.'

'Nor to me, but there's been violence again. Once against Oliver Raden and now against a contact of the girl's.' He considered, then added thoughtfully: 'You did better than you knew to tail Miss Raden. So stay with her till twelve o'clock.'

'Why twelve o'clock?'

'Because at noon they're going to pull her in. Our friends the police have been perfectly frank. They can't leave that safe-blowing up in the air for ever.'

'I see. A pity.' Mary Maguffy clearly thought it was a pity.

'And another thing too. With any sort of luck at all they'll get enough from the girl to run Oliver in as well. Not at once, I should say—it will take a few hours. But they're bound to take him too quite soon.'

'What do I do?'

'You don't interfere. In a way it rather suits us. If either or both are in danger again they'll be safer in a police station than in that flat. Keep me fully in the picture.'

'Right.'

Mary Maguffy put the radio into her handbag again. She went back into the supermarket, looking round quickly for Sheila Raden. She'd been buying bread but now was not. Mary made certain she'd left the market, then considered her own next move. Sheila would still be marketing but Mary didn't know her shopping-round and the odds against picking her up again were long. It would be futile to hunt for her blindly, but nor could Mary just lose her, that wouldn't be professional, so she'd go to the flat and make sure she'd returned. That was the only course when once she'd lost her.

She began to step out briskly for Sheila's duplex.

Sheila Raden had left the supermarket laden with provisions for two days, French bread, oil and cheese, an almost continental shopping-bag for a man without notable appetite but fastidious about what he ate. She already had meat and vegetables and was considerably burdened. She looked round for a taxi and didn't see one, but as she started to walk one drew up beside her. She went to it quickly and spoke to the driver.

'Will you take me when you've finished, please?'

The young man who'd got out of the taxi had paid the driver, and now to her surprise he used her name.

'Miss Raden?'

She nodded.

'I thought I might find you shopping. I've been looking for you everywhere.'

She didn't know him but could place him, the well made but consciously country clothes, suède brogues and the hat half a size too small. The accent too—it was careful but it betrayed him. It was the accent of a leading man in musical comedy of the twenties, the speech of an Englishman who'd been born in Shahbaddin and reared there. He'd be one of the British colony there and Sheila disliked it heartily.

'Oh yes?' she said.

He began to talk fast—too fast, she thought. 'I'm from the High Commissioner's office and I've a very important message for you.'

'You could have telephoned.'

'I did but nobody answered.'

She knew this was a lie and she felt uneasy. Oliver didn't go out but he answered the telephone. She started to move to the taxi but another woman had taken it. At a loss for how to cope with him she said:

'Then you'd better give me the message, whatever it is.'

'I can't, it's too complicated.' He gave her a smile—she loathed it. It was meant to be easy and reassuring but came out as plain ingratiating, the smile of a salesman flogging flat-irons to a housewife. 'If you'll come to the High Commission we can explain.'

'I've never been there in my life.'

'There's got to be a first time, hasn't there?'

His manner had changed and Sheila noticed it. She didn't know what was happening but she knew she mistrusted this strange young man. . . . Telephone calls which hadn't been made, chasing her on her shopping. And what sort of message could that wet of a High Commissioner have? Even if he had one, why not write first? Sending young men to pester her. . . .

She turned on her heel but he put a hand on her arm. His grip was surprisingly strong. . . . Drop the basket and try to hit him? Make a scene in the street and she hated scenes? She hesitated and he spun her.

She felt the stab in her free arm and gasped. He was putting something into his pocket. It looked like a tube of glass. She began to run but at once he grabbed her, holding her round the waist, his face against hers. She knew there were passers-by but they wouldn't be overly curious. This wasn't a part of London where public kissing raised a scandal. She could hear him counting quietly, backwards, and he seemed to have started at five. Five, four, three, two. . . .

As she went limp a black saloon drew alongside. Another man got out and they pushed her in. The car drove away.

On the pavement a man said 'Stop,' but much too late.

Mary Maguffy walked quickly to Sheila's duplex and rang the bell. To Oliver who answered she said pleasantly: 'May I come in?'

'Of course. Mrs Maguffy, isn't it?'

148

He gave her a welcoming social smile but she could see that he was miserable. It was early still and Sheila hadn't yet done the housework. There were bedclothes on the divan still and Mary Maguffy observed them. Another pity, she thought, though perhaps not now a pressing one. If the police were coming for Sheila at noon she'd have more important matters on hand than how many beds she chose to make up. Oliver folded the bedclothes neatly, putting them over the back of a chair. He waved at the divan.

'Please sit down. Can I offer you a drink?' He still had a little whisky left since he used it very seldom and could drug himself on next to nothing.

'Thank you, it's much too early. I only looked in to ask a question.'

'Yes?'

'Where's Miss Raden?'

'She went out shopping.'

'I did know that.'

He looked at her shrewdly. 'So you were tailing her and lost her.'

'That's right.' She answered quite composedly, she'd been doing a job which she wasn't ashamed of. 'I was told to watch the pair of you, so as I knew you stayed here I went off with Miss Raden. Then I lost her in a supermarket and came back here to pick up the trail.'

'To pick up the trail?'

'That was really rather clumsy. I mean to make sure she'd come back to the flat.'

His expression clouded. 'I can understand your watching me. But Sheila . . . You don't imagine . . .?'

She didn't answer but asked a question again. 'What time did she go out?'

'About a quarter to ten.'

Mary looked at the clock. She'd lost Sheila Raden at ten fifteen and it was now coming up for the half-hour past. 'How long does the shopping take her?'

'I really don't know but she's usually pretty quick. Say half an hour—forty minutes at most. You're not telling me, you're not thinking . . .?'

She managed a smile but for the second time didn't answer. 'Do you mind if I wait?'

'I'd like you to wait.'

They sat in a tension which steadily mounted. Ten forty, ten fifty and five to eleven. Neither spoke but both smoked fiercely. The ormulu clock on the mantelshelf chimed eleven. Oliver said explosively: 'I'm going out to find her.'

'Useless. If anything should have happened you'll be much too late to help her, and if it hasn't she'll turn up here in her own good time.'

'You really don't think——'

The telephone rang sharply.

Oliver was out of his chair at once, picking up the receiver, turning his lean profile.

'Sheila?' he said eagerly.

A man's voice answered. Mary couldn't hear the words but the voice was a man's quite certainly. It seemed to be making a statement of fact.

'Impossible,' Oliver Raden said.

Mary Maguffy was watching his face. For a second it had fallen apart but he had it under control again. The voice in the receiver seemed to be repeating a previous statement.

Oliver said: 'But she's never been there in her life.'

This time the voice was louder and Mary Maguffy caught the words. 'Well, she's here now.'

'Oh God.'

The voice went back to a menacing murmur and Oliver, rigid and silent, listened. At the end there was clearly a question, for Oliver said curtly: 'Say that again.'

The telephone did so.

There was a moment of indecision, of utter agony Mary could sense and share. Then Oliver said: 'I'll come at once.' He hung up and returned to Mary Maguffy. 'That,' he said flatly, 'was the High Commissioner's office. A man called Kin.'

'I know about Kin. I was given your file before that business at the Stag, and since then I've been told the whole story.'

'He's got Sheila in his office.'

Mary thought quickly, then asked on a rising note he couldn't miss: 'Would she have gone there voluntarily?'

'No, I don't think so.'

'Then he's snatched her.' Mary started to make for the telephone but Oliver Raden waved her down.

'That isn't all.'

She sat down reluctantly but there was something which made her. This was a man and she a woman. Again she watched his face but she couldn't read it. Only one thing and that was clear. Oliver Raden was sick with fear but behind the fear was something else and the something else would drive him. Courage, she thought—it was harder than gold.

. . . That bloody gold.

He was explaining to her quietly. 'Sheila's bait, they're not interested. It's me they want and if I go there they'll release her.'

'You can't believe that.'

'I don't.'

'I know a reason they might want you.'

'Yes, so do I.' He was looking at his hands, she saw. A shudder shook him.

'Or even one worse if you call it worse. They could simply want you out of the way. From their point of view you're the principal danger.'

'I've thought of that too.'

'You're not going, of course.'

'I rather think I'll have to.' He asked her almost innocently: 'Tell me, would *you* go?'

'No, I would not.'

'You'd be perfectly right but the circumstances are different. You're brave, you see.'

'Fiddle.'

'But you've never had to hide your fear. Of yourself, I mean —that's another sort of torture.'

'Any man who's had what you have, any man who risks the same again——'

'I know—that's only sensible. But I've got to go.' He was silent, thinking grimly. 'If I run into any trouble could the Executive ever help me?'

'Perhaps, but not quickly. A High Commission ranks as an embassy. That means it's technically foreign territory.'

'How long?'

'Charles Russell being the man he is I'd say forty-eight hours. But that's at best.'

He repeated it. 'Forty-eight hours.' He was looking at his hands again and once again he shivered.

'You don't have to go, it's utter madness.'

'You needn't tell me that.'

'Don't go.' She was almost weeping.

'I must.' He gave her a smile which shattered her. 'It's my only chance.'

'Of what?'

'Of happiness,' he said.

He rose and Mary with him. Once she had worn a uniform and she was wishing that she wore it now. In uniform you saluted a brave man. Instead of saluting she kissed him shyly.

'Good luck.'

'That's kind. Would you like to stay and telephone?' He picked up a light overcoat, walking to the door with it. It's turned surprisingly cold,' he said.

The door shut behind him firmly.

Mary didn't use the telephone but pulled her radio from her bag instead. When she had finished Charles Russell said immediately:

'Get here and fast.'

Oliver Raden paid off his taxi, walking up the steps to the High Commission's front door. He rang the bell and gave his name and a Chinese porter admitted him.

'Mr Kin is expecting me.'

He was shown to a pompously furnished room and there he was left to wait alone. He wasn't afraid now but simply numb.

He wasn't even curious. He read an out-of-date *Country Life* without knowing the words.

Two men came in so quietly that at first he hardly heard them. One stood behind his chair, the other in front. The one in front was Mr Kin. He said with a triumph he wasn't hiding:

'I knew you'd come.'

Oliver Raden rose and turned. The man behind the chair was white and Oliver could place him just as accurately as had Sheila. So the British in Shahbaddin were ratting too.

He felt a brutal pain at the base of his skull, collapsing as Kin caught him.

He woke an hour later, bound and gagged, again in the dark and again sick with fear. He'd been kept in the dark once before and he knew what followed. Not that he was in pain again yet. He could almost wish he were for it might have helped. He was on the upper of two bunks and on the lower something was stirring.

He heard a woman's stifled sobbing.

CHAPTER THIRTEEN

Mr Kin was talking to his High Commissioner again, and this time he wasn't troubling with the 'Your Excellencies', nor even with normal politeness. He was under pressure and hadn't time for it. The High Commissioner was saying miserably:

'But it's an appallingly dangerous plan.'

Kin looked at him without pity. His Excellency had sold his race for a mess of potage, more precisely for life in a great capitalist city, the woman in Shepherd's Bush, the club in Pall Mall. He was therefore to be despised and Kin despised him. But he was also rather stupid and that was worse. The price of his defection had been the promise to leave him in London. Did he seriously think it would ever be honoured? Kin knew it would not be, and a man who could think otherwise was the most extravagant kind of optimist. The High Commissioner would be quietly recalled, His Excellency wouldn't live long. Kin's party had no employment for men who sold out for material gain. 'It's been decided,' Kin said coldly.

'But surely it's quite unnecessary. With the news as it is from Shahbaddin, that message this morning—you saw it too. Sayed . . .' The High Commissioner choked, recovered himself with an effort; he said more or less lucidly: 'Why do we have to bother with a pair of wretched Radens?'

'You know about the gold and you always did. Even from the beginning. You knew it was gold we wanted but you decided to go to law about some jewels in a Raden safe.' Kin almost spat at him. 'The law—the bourgeois law. The ally of our enemies.'

'It seemed the best way to start the search. And we had it confirmed from Shahbaddin.'

'By your friends, by my enemies. Now *your* enemies, remember.'

The High Commissioner was weeping now and Kin watched him with impatience. Tears wasted time and he hadn't a great deal of it. Kin opened his mouth but his senior beat him to it.

'Do you still believe that gold exists?'

'I obey my instructions till they're changed or withdrawn.'

'But how could the Radens reach it now? Even supposing they did, how could it matter? If Sayed's just done what that message said——'

'Be quiet,' Kin snapped. He wasn't prepared to explain, he wouldn't try. The High Commissioner was an alien, almost a different species of man. What did he know of a burning faith, of a lifelong commitment, of rigid discipline? It would be impossible to make him see, the grossest waste of time to try. 'My first orders were to get the gold. I've failed in that but I still have orders. They're to make quite sure that the Radens don't succeed where I have failed.'

'But with things as they are, Sayed now in the capital . . . Haven't you any discretion about your orders?'

'No.'

The High Commissioner was hating it but he brought himself at last to ask the question. 'What are you going to do?'

Kin told him.

'Not here.' The voice was terrified.

'No, of course not here. They'll be taken away discreetly and just as discreetly dealt with. In quite another country. You needn't worry.'

'But you can't abduct them forcibly. This may be a High Commission and the London police won't come breaking in, but smuggling people out has been tried before. The least sign of duress at any airport——'

'Who's talking about duress?'

'Aren't you?'

'I am not. I might have had to consider it but they've made it quite unnecessary. I've talked to them separately and one thing's quite certain. The least threat to one and the other will do as he's told.'

'Why should he?'

'Because,' Kin said, 'they're both in love.' He pronounced the word with extreme distaste. Sex was necessary to an efficient life and a man couldn't give his best if he were seriously deprived of it. But love was a bourgeois luxury, a weakness. He was grateful for its existence though, since he meant to exploit it fully; he said once again: 'Any serious pressure on either and the other will do at they're told. So I've booked seats on a plane this evening and our friends will be taking them quietly. Young Layton will be going too but I'm sure there'll be no trouble at Heathrow. Layton's duties will come later. . . . Passports? They haven't got them of course, but they're our nationals still and I've issued others.' Kin pulled two from his pocket. 'Everything has been thought of, even a little luggage.'

'And then?' the High Commissioner asked. He hadn't wished to but the words had come.

'You really wish to know what then?'

'No, no, no, no.'

In the Security Executive there were three men and a woman round Russell's table. None had had luncheon and all had forgone it gladly. Russell made the two introductions necessary. 'You all know each other except Patterson. Mary, this is James Patterson, a Deputy Chief Officer of the London Fire Brigade—Patterson, this is Mary Maguffy. The man behind a beard denies a name since he's rather eminent, but he also advises what we call our Research and Special. You can say anything to either which you could also say to me.'

They all sat down and Russell began to explain. 'I'll try and keep it as short as I can. In its simplest form two people I'm interested in have been kidnapped and detained, or to be accurate the woman was kidnapped and the man then went after her. They're prisoners in the High Commission of a State which is in the Commonwealth.'

The Fire Chief nodded. 'I can see that would be tricky.'

'Very tricky indeed. I should add two things. The first is that I won't let myself think what may be happening to them as we sit here talking. The other is that I'm personally involved. *Personally*. This man and this woman were under my protection. My duties, such as they are, apart, I would rather resign than leave them to their fates, which could be unexplained disappearance and then God help them. I much dislike melodrama so I must assure you I'm not indulging it.' Russell looked at James Patterson. 'But I owe it to you to be honest. Am I also being clear?'

'Perfectly clear, and I sympathize. I'm glad I don't have your job.'

'Then I needn't tell any of you that High Commissions rank as embassies and in theory are foreign territory. The police couldn't work on a search warrant even if they could get one in time, but the fiction of extraterritoriality isn't absolute. It can't be absolute in practice because the building is in fact in another State. That State retains its residual rights and they've been pretty well studied in the profession I happen to work in. So I'll give you two examples, of which the first is infectious disease. If the Patagonian Embassy were harbouring cases of plague you could in extremity do something about it, but you'd have to have watertight evidence which we certainly don't have here, and there'd be the usual paper war of doctors' certificates and the rest of it. But you can protect your own citizens if an embassy's action is endangering them sufficiently. Or its lack of action. Or perhaps its sheer misfortune. That's basically the law, though the diplomatists say it goes further. Naturally they would.'

'Did you mention sheer misfortune?'

Charles Russell nodded.

'Such as catching on fire,' the Fire Chief said calmly. 'Was that going to be your second example?' He didn't speak accusingly but was as matter-of-fact as the Scot he was. His appearance of dourness could be decidedly deceptive, for he had the pawky humour of his native town and also its sense of a personal obligation. Which he wouldn't have denied he bore to Russell. Indeed he was devoted to him and had excellent reason to be so since Russell had saved his son's career. He'd been a civil servant rising rapidly and his work had been what in the jargon was called sensitive. Also he'd made the most foolish of contacts and his superiors had heard of them. So had his father and he'd gone straightaway to Russell. Who had called the boy up and scared him severely. He was ready to back his private judgement and his judgement of this young man had been that he was foolish but not dangerous. He could become that in time—they were clever at entangling men—but for the moment he wasn't awash beyond recall. So he had left Russell's office extremely white and that had been the end of it. Russell had regarded it as a morning well spent. There were at least four Members of Parliament whom he knew but couldn't announce were committed communists, and when that was the way the country was the Head of the Executive had a choice of serious game to hunt. As an official it gave him no pleasure, as a man no satisfaction at all to crucify the small fry.

Russell hadn't been thinking of bread on the waters when he'd rescued James Patterson's promising son; he had by now almost forgotten it. James Patterson never had and never would. He was saying again coolly:

'Such as catching on fire.' If 'catching' had been emphasized the emphasis had been almost unnoticeable. 'I should perhaps make it clear that I'm not present and never have been. I came on a bus when I got your call, and saw nobody I knew either on it or off. So I'm a ghost but I'll answer questions. But the fewer the better—you'll understand that.'

'Then I hope the first won't sound too brutal. If you saw an embassy burning what would you do?'

'Our duty,' the Fire Chief said promptly, 'though it would have to be a proper fire. We don't go bashing our way in, embassy or anything else, because a chimney's on fire and some nervous clerk calls us. But if we saw a real fire, something which looked like spreading and endangering other property, we wouldn't pay much attention to a man on the doorstep who tried to stop us.'

'Whatever reason he gave?'

'There wouldn't be time for argument if the fire looked likely to spread. Where is this High Commission?'

'In the Kensington Road.'

'That makes it easier, it's one of our black spots. Oldish Victorian houses with lots of wood. The local men are scared stiff of it. They wouldn't waste much time with a coloured man shouting the odds about diplomatic privilege; they'd go in first and leave headquarters to parley later. And quite right too in an old and crowded area. Which brings me to another point, though officially I'm not here still. I beg you—don't overdo it.'

'We won't.' Russell waved at the man with the beard. 'Your turn to talk.'

The man behind the beard had the air of the top-class boffin, the same precise speech. He spoke for two minutes and then stopped dead; he'd said everything he wished to say and wuffling much annoyed him. James Patterson didn't comment but cocked an inquiring eye at Russell. Russell returned the look composedly, one senior official to another.

'You mustn't ask me about the details but I'm entitled to judge the technicians who help us.'

The scientist inclined his head but didn't speak. It was a compliment and a deserved one but he wasn't interested in small talk with men he regarded as depressingly uneducated.

The Fire Chief said: 'I see,' and thought. 'But I ought to warn you of one thing. You'll be sending in one of your own people no doubt, but you can't mix strangers with the crews from a local station. They know each other far too well.'

'I'd thought of a Woman Auxiliary.'

'Who don't normally go to fires, I'm afraid.'

'I know. But they go on exercises and they have to do their regular drills.' Russell stared at the ceiling. 'So a Woman Auxiliary, clean and tidy of course, correctly dressed, will be walking along the Kensington Road at half-past five precisely. She happens to see a fire, and human nature being what it is——'

'What she did would be irregular but it would also be very natural. It wouldn't excite much comment at the time.' The Fire Chief looked at Mary Maguffy. She liked the look for it wasn't surprised. It was a cool appraising stare and seemed approving. She was grateful for that and to Russell too. She knew very well that he had men better qualified, but once you were on a job you saw it through. It was one of Charles Russell's established rules and not the least reason his staff served him happily.

James Patterson added: 'The uniform?'

'We can manage the uniform.'

'At half-past five, I think you said?' He was making a tidy note in a neat diary.

'I'd like it very much earlier, but there's the staff work to be organized, the box of tricks, its delivery by hand——'

'I understand the urgency but the time is entirely for you.' The Fire Chief rose. 'The Kensington Road can be on my way home, so at half-past five I'll be driving along it. If I happen to see a fire what more natural than that I should stop for it?' He smiled faintly at Mary Maguffy. 'Even more natural than a Woman Auxiliary who sees the chance of a lifetime to get in on a real job. Naturally she takes it. Equally naturally she wouldn't shout her name. If she isn't obtrusive she'll simply be forgotten, perhaps not even noticed much. She won't be obtrusive, will she?'

'No.'

'Nor shall I since I'll be in mufti. But I might conceivably be useful.' James Patterson turned to Russell. 'There's a gentleman's understanding that you won't be burning the street down?'

'Of course.'

'But firemen aren't quite fools, you know.' He was suddenly very dour indeed. 'I think you mentioned a box of tricks, and if I should happen to notice what as a fireman I shouldn't wish to see . . .'

He let the sentence float but Russell didn't. 'Thank you,' he said simply.

'The normal answer is "For nothing", and nothing is what it emphatically is since I'm not even here to listen.' James Patterson walked to the door and collected his hat. His dourness suddenly fell from him; he looked round the room and his smile was almost merry. 'Charming people,' he said. 'I must really contrive to meet you sometime.'

He tapped his bowler hat and went out.

For Charles Russell the next few hours meant intensive work, but by five the details were complete, the orders given. He wasn't too happy to have it so for action had been an opiate and the last thing he wanted was time to think. If Chief Superintendent Willis hadn't been pulling in Sheila at noon, if he himself hadn't radioed Mary Maguffy when she'd been doing her job of shadowing Sheila, if he hadn't obliged her to call back in private and break her watch, if Oliver hadn't gone after Sheila, a mad thing to do, to walk knowingly into an open trap, a bad mad stupid splendid thing . . . If, if, if—the devil's word. Now a man might be under torture again. Battle, murder and sudden death were tolerable: Russell had seen all three and subconsciously had accepted them. He'd have broken if he had not. But torture, no. It was a barbarian regression, increasing daily in its use. The skin of civilization was thin enough in any case, and this was the ugliest crack of his sixty years. He simply couldn't stomach it, he'd never allowed its use and never would. The extremes of mental pressure when they were necessary: Charles Russell had a job to do and a public conscience to do it with, but he also had a private one and in the matter of torture the latter came first. He felt sick as he looked at the clock. It was now ten past five and Raden had gone there at round about eleven. . . .

Russell disciplined his thoughts but not quite wholly. There was Sheila Raden too. He didn't fear they'd torture her since they hadn't an obvious motive, but her name was Raden, her background immutable—private property, the class enemy, the woman who lived but hadn't the right to. For Russell had dutifully read it all, equipping himself to think as the other

161

half thought. So there was the capitalist young woman, the parasite on the grim new world. Perhaps. They had a very good case and he wouldn't deny it. But also the young woman who'd been courteous to an older man, delicately offering him the illusion that he was almost a contemporary, though one with more to offer than a mere boy. Was that quite contemptible? Perhaps again but Russell thought not. So you weighed the two women and God held the balance.

God held it finally but Russell was in this here and now. Personally, inescapably, since he'd held out protection and the shield had been cracked contemptuously. It hadn't been hyperbole when he'd been talking to James Patterson. He had said he would rather resign than turn his back, and that had been the literal truth. From somewhere in Russell's subconscious mind a word bubbled up and broke surface crudely. Consciously he rejected it since it wasn't the sort of word he used, but privately he knew it was just. This was a matter of honour.

He saw that his secretary had come in quietly. 'The Minister has been ringing you.'

Russell looked at a coloured telephone. 'Why can't he ring on the proper line?'

'I see you've disconnected it.'

'So I have. What is it he wants?'

'It was something about Shahbaddin. There's been news and he wanted to give it.'

'Tell him I'm in conference or any rubbish that occurs to you. Tell him I'll ring him back when I'm free.'

Russell's secretary went to do so but almost at once was back again. Charles Russell raised his eyebrows but didn't speak. He was on a knife-edge of racking tension, he would have liked to drink but didn't dare, but he'd known this woman ten years and more. She in turn knew his own moods perfectly; she wouldn't have interrupted again if she hadn't been very sure of the need.

'A message has just come in and they thought you should see it at once.' She handed him a typewritten sheet. Russell read the first three lines indifferently but not indifferently thereafter. His taut face relaxed.

It was a message from a source he trusted, and the story at its shortest was that the man they called Sayed now controlled Shahbaddin. Russell heard himself laugh and this evening he hadn't expected to. The operation had been a classic, a Staff College exercise in the almost bloodless revolution. A dozen men had walked in on the capital's only broadcasting station, another dozen on Posts and Telegraphs. They'd been armed but they hadn't fired a shot; they hadn't had need to fire a shot. The only shooting had been in the suburbs, where three Chinese Ministers, one Chinese editor, had been keeping illegal bodyguards which had resisted their masters' arrests with guns. There'd been quite sharp but localized fighting between two detachments of men with modern weapons, but the fighting had spread to no other quarter, had indeed been the exception against a background of that supremely effective tool, the passive crowd. Russell had laughed aloud again for this was something he understood and had seen. Not a riot which could be a challenge, but thousands and thousands of people in the streets. You packed the main streets with bodies and that was that. Tear-gas and armoured cars might thin them temporarily, but a peaceful crowd which knew its own strength was the ultimate weapon in anything but a dictatorship. The police could do nothing but brown it and the Shahbaddin police wouldn't brown their own people, even if they'd been ordered to which quite clearly they had not. The police had in fact been neutral, perhaps fore-knowing. There was something called the army, in practice a battalion of police more heavily armed, but that had stayed in barracks. When Sayed had come on the air it had marched out smartly, formed up and cheered. The rest of the police had declared for him already.

Russell's secretary returned with a second sheet. On the air Sayed had been magnificent. He hadn't come as a dictator, he said ('They all say that, they always have') and there were going to be fresh elections just as soon as it was possible ('They have to say that too for consumption in the United States').

Meanwhile he thanked his friends and invited others. He wasn't head of a party but of a movement. All were welcome beneath his banner, Malay, Chinese . . .

A storm of cheers.

. . . Malay, Chinese, the European colony. All were welcome upon a single qualification. And that was loyalty, loyalty to Shahbaddin. There'd been men who put their race before their country, men who'd been taking orders from a nameless but foreign Power, even men who had used illegal arms when the day of reckoning came for them. All these would be punished where they hadn't died already. . . .

A sudden swift silence.

. . . but no man need fear who put his country first and not another. No man, no woman, no creed, no race——

'Shahbaddin, Shabaddin.'

It sounded wonderful stuff, Charles Russell thought, marvellous meaty popular stuff, much more effective than any ex-professor could reasonably be expected to keep on tap, even an ex-professor who had just achieved a successful political take-over. But Russell had little time to relish it. He rang to Communications, telling them to net him to Mary Maguffy at once. It was five twenty-five and she'd be sitting in a discreet black car, waiting to start her precisely timed walk. He hated talking on radio telephones, mistrusting the mystique of it, the I Say Agains, the Overs and Outs, all the overplayed conventions. But he'd learnt how to use them effectively; he would rap out a couple of sentences, then wait for the comment or answer. It wasn't a method for ripe Augustan dialogue but it communicated beautifully. When Mary came through he barked:

'There's been a small change of plan but nothing to worry about.'

'Yes?' She knew the form.

'Your instructions were to get them both out, then to take them to the flat and await further orders.'

'Correct.'

'Amended as follows. Before taking them anywhere you will give them some information.'

'Pass it.'

'There's been a revolution in Shahbaddin. It is now controlled by a man called Sayed.'

'Is it indeed?'

'You sound surprised.'

'I'm surprised. He'll be delighted and so will she.'

'You think so?'

'I'm sure of it. I've seen them together.' A pause. 'Not happy in England. Homesick. Also in love.'

Russell said serenely: 'I bow to a woman's judgement.'

'So?'

'So if they react as you expect they will you can give them a piece of further news. Which is that an aircraft is at their immediate disposal. You know which one.'

'You've alerted it?'

'Not yet—I will.'

'I think they'll both take it. He'll have reason to get back again and the girl will follow him happily. Am I to go with them?'

'No.'

'But I'm to take them to the airfield?'

'No again. I can't risk your being seen together. Who's your driver?'

She told him.

'Good. Tell him what I've just told you. He's to pass it on when they reach the car. Getting them there is solely for you.'

'I'll do my best.'

'I know.'

Russell switched off, then connected a coloured telephone on his desk. He rang an airfield near London and spoke decisively. When he had finished an efficient and practical voice said simply: 'Right.'

The unexpected bout of action had released the worst of his tension. Russell decided that a drink would now be in order. Half-way through it he noticed the time and smiled. It was twenty to six and in the Kensington Road there would be action of a different kind.

CHAPTER FOURTEEN

The messenger was smartly dressed, the parcel an impressive one, tied with official-looking tape and sealed with an indeterminate but evidently important seal. It was addressed to the Head of Chancery, marked *Immediate* and *By Hand*, and the porter at the High Commissioner's office took it upstairs unhesitatingly.

The Head of Chancery was a Malay but with a corruptive dash of Indian, and it was coming up for half-past five. Like his master the High Commissioner he had compensations for exile in London and an appointment with the prettiest of them at a quarter to six that evening. He sighed as he glanced at the clock, but the parcel looked official and he wasn't without a vestigial conscience. He took a paper knife and cut the tape; he then bent down and broke the seal.

There was a very faint explosion, no more than a champagne cork, and the lid of the cardboard box sprang up into his face. For a second he was blinded and didn't quite see what happened next; he had an impression of jets of some colourless liquid spurting outwards in four directions. The lid fell to the floor but he didn't pick it up. He stood staring instead for the room was burning fiercely. The curtains were blazing, the carpet was a spreading pool of flame. The parcel itself was disintegrating as he looked at it, but belching out smoke, a dense acrid smoke which made him cough. With what was later commended as courage he ran to the window tearing at the curtains, opening the casement. He shouted: 'Fire, fire, fire,' as the smoke poured past him solidly. He then retreated to the landing where he was sick.

On the opposite side of the Kensington Road a man had been leaning against the railings of the Park. He began to move immediately, running with purpose since he knew exactly where to run to. In the telephone box he began to dial—not Nine-Nine-Nine since that wasted time, but the number of the nearest fire station. He gave the address of the fire and two pieces of information. There was a great deal of smoke coming out of an open window, flames behind, and a wog had been leaning out and yelling his head off.

Outside the High Commission there was already a small but curious crowd, forming in the way of crowds, out of nothing but inevitability. A single policeman was trying to move it on, talking about obstruction to the firemen when they arrived. The crowd shuffled but reformed again. It could already hear the insistent bells as the engines fought their way through the evening traffic. There was a formidable cloud of smoke and the show was free.

Upstairs in the High Commission there was the panic the boffin had counted on. He'd promised he wouldn't start a too serious fire and had fixed it for much more smoke than flame, something which a competent fire crew could kill in minutes. But he'd also been assured in terms that the staff of the High Commission was unlikely to behave competently. These assurances had been justified. The Chancery was empty now but on the landing outside there was total chaos, a roar of contradictory advice, an increasing *mêlée* of purposeless bodies. The door onto the landing had been left open when the Malay had fled, and though somebody had an extinguisher now the acid smoke drove him back at once. Coughing and gasping they backed in disorder across the landing towards the stairs.

From the room next to Chancery the connecting door opened. Kin stood on the threshold, he stood dismayed. . . . Fight it? He knew where the apparatus was kept but it hadn't been used or checked in years, for there was a fixed annual grant to maintain the building and Kin was aware which pocket received what wasn't spent. Besides, he could hear a noise in the street, the engines arriving and a commotion in the hall. He started to choke as the wall of smoke caught him.

He went back into his own small room, shutting the door behind him, sitting to think. Kin had never been in a fire before and couldn't judge one. It looked serious though, the smoke told him that, and he had papers in his wall safe which His Excellency didn't know about. Suppose they couldn't control it, suppose it spread. The safe would be fireproof, that wasn't his worry, but if the house went up there'd be a pile of smoking rubble and somewhere in that pile Kin's safe. He could probably recover it but suppose he didn't. Suppose, just suppose, that a prowling policeman became too curious. Much more serious, suppose that the Security Executive . . . A safe in a foreign embassy's ruins, the secret telegrams, the codes. . . . A swift little skilful man before Kin himself could get to it. . . . It was good, that damned Executive. And he couldn't take his papers home. That was Rule One, inviolable.

So he'd be forced to destroy them, there wasn't an alternative in the time he had to work in. It was exceedingly inconvenient but he couldn't accept the other risk. One didn't accept that sort of risk after years of conditioning, training. Kin lit the fire in the grate, then walked across to the safe and spun the dials. He opened the door. The most important ones first. . . .

The hair on the nape of his neck rose stiffly. He swung on his heel. A man had been standing behind him. Kin hadn't heard him come in but he knew him well.

He also knew he was going to die.

The crowd outside the High Commission was a little disappointed. It had hoped for dramatic rescues on ladders, but though smoke was still pouring densely from a first-floor window it was clear that the fire was already under control. Two machines had arrived promptly and the crews had a hose through the open front door. There wouldn't be any melodrama and the crowd began to melt away, but there was a good deal of bustle and Mary Maguffy, correctly uniformed, slipped in without challenge. She'd been warned to be unobtrusive and she was.

She had made her plan and now acted on it smoothly. It

had been Russell's view that Sheila and Oliver Raden would be in one of two places, the cellars or the attics, and Mary had tossed for first look and the cellars had won. Inside the house there was still an uproar, a babel of tongues which she didn't know and an elderly man whom she took to be His Excellency wringing his hands and weeping. Mary paid him no attention but looked for the inevitable green baize door to the servants' quarters. She opened and went through it with an air of brisk authority, and at once found the stairs she had hoped for and expected. She went down them at the double.

She found herself in a stone-flagged hall, surprisingly cold, lit by a grating to the courtyard outside. Three doors let out of it and she tried the first. . . . A lumber room—nothing. The second was the wine cellar but the third was locked. She called but nobody answered.

Mary Maguffy inspected the lock. She could pick it but she hadn't the time. She took from her uniform shoulder-bag a small plastic box. One side was metal, magnetized, and she clicked it against the doorlock, pressing the top left-hand corner where the boffin had told her to press. Ten seconds, he'd said. . . .

She went into the wine cellar, crouching but not frightened. She shared Russell's simple faith in his high-class boffin.

The noise of the limpet was louder than she'd expected, the unmistakable crack of high explosive. It shook the bottles in their cradles and she had a second to think how Charles Russell would have deplored it. Mary went back into the hall again. The third door was sagging crookedly now and she pushed it open fully. She felt for the light switch but the explosion had broken the bulb. She used her torch.

There was a two-tiered bunk and two bodies had been tied to it. Both moved as she touched them.

. . . So at least they're alive.

Mary began on the lower, freeing Sheila, cutting the rope with the knife she'd brought, then easing the taped gag carefully. Sheila Raden put her legs down and Mary helped her upright. She stood for a second, then fell in a heap. Mary picked her up again. She was clearly very shaken but there weren't any signs of injury. Mary said: 'They haven't . . .?'

'They've been threatening me, and Oliver too.' She looked at the upper bunk. 'Be quick.'

They cut Oliver free in turn and he climbed down stiffly. Mary saw that he was uninjured too but she didn't like the look of him. He was composed—too composed. He stretched deliberately like a waking dog. 'So it's Mrs Maguffy—I'd hoped it might be.' He was talking to Mary but evidently not considering her. 'How do I ever thank you?'

'You don't, you listen. Now. Get out of here and both of you. At once. If anyone tries to stop you don't be stopped. When you're out in the street turn left and left again. Down Ennismore Gardens, and there's a cul-de-sac on the left again. There'll be a big black car with a driver wearing goggles. He's got a message for you, an important one. . . .'

She was talking to Sheila Raden alone but a voice from half-way up the stairs was shouting down. 'Send Sheila on, I'll follow.' The stone treads echoed Oliver Raden's running feet.

Mary Maguffy frowned, alarmed. She had her hunch and it scared her. This wasn't a moment for moral judgements but it was emphatically one for working to plan. She couldn't blame Oliver Raden if he was seeking to settle a private score but she could curse him to the four winds of hell if he embroiled the Executive in the sort of violent scrape it abhorred. She rapped at Sheila Raden: 'Go to the car.'

'Alone?' Sheila was still shaky but nevertheless she had hesitated.

'Do as I say. I'll send him.'

'Promise?'

'I promise.' It was a rash one but Mary would do her best. She ran up the steps after Oliver Raden. Her hunch hadn't lessened.

The firemen had the fire out now but the Chancery was a reeking shambles. Mary didn't go in—he wouldn't be there—and it would be pointless to risk an encounter she'd have to explain to some curious fireman. Oliver Raden's intention she thought she knew and she'd have to stop him. There were several doors off the landing. She opened the first.

Two unarmed men were fighting savagely, one short, one tall. They weren't very good at unarmed combat, but Mary had seen men fight before and the fact that neither was expert didn't deceive her. They were fighting to kill and one would die. The first to go down would not get up.

The tall one fell suddenly as the wicked knee caught him, gasping, defenceless. But the other didn't follow him down to strangle. Instead he ran to the desk and opened a drawer. He had a gun out now and was pointing it. Mary Maguffy heard the safety catch click to Fire.

Sheila walked up the stairs from the cellar, her legs coming back to her. She hadn't wished to leave alone but she wasn't stupid. Like Mary she had sensed something, something unplanned and probably unwelcome. The almost physical smell of violence was in the air. Another woman would be a nuisance then, might even make things worse than they were. If anyone could help Oliver it would be Mary Maguffy alone.

In the hall when she reached it there was still some confusion, enough for her passage to raise no challenge. There was a man who was holding a neat bowler hat and she thought that he looked at her curiously. But he didn't accost her. A group of firemen was blocking the wide front door, but the man with the bowler hat gave an order as she approached them. They moved away to comply with it and Sheila was in the open air.

She gulped at it gratefully, walking fast to her left and left again. . . . Yes, a cul-de-sac and a big black car. A polite young man in goggles and chauffeur's uniform opened the door and when he'd settled her passed an envelope. 'I think you should read this at once,' he said.

There were only six lines in Mary's scrawl and Sheila read them more than once. At first they didn't mean a lot but then, as the message bit, they almost broke her. She said weakly to the young driver:

'Do you know what this letter says?'
'I do.'
'You work for the Executive too?'
'In my modest way it employs me.' She liked his smile.
'But this changes everything,' Sheila said.
'If you wanted it to it certainly could.'
'It's the truth about Shahbaddin?'
'It'd be an awfully silly lie you could check in an evening paper.'
'And this aircraft would really take us there?'
'By stages, yes. But you'd find it was all laid on.'
'Both of us?'
'Certainly.'
'Oh God,' Sheila said, 'if he doesn't get out of that dreadful house——'
'Why isn't he with you—did something go wrong?'
'I don't know. Mary Maguffy freed us both. . . . We started talking. . . . She told us to come here, both of us, then Oliver suddenly wasn't there. He ran upstairs and I'm afraid for what he may try to do. He's suffered a lot.'
'I've heard.' The young chauffeur took her hand and squeezed it, but unamorously. 'Do you want to go back to Shahbaddin?'
'More than anything else in the world.'
'And he?'
She managed a smile though it wasn't a big one. 'If I go so will Oliver.'
The driver considered. 'You say he ran upstairs alone?'
She nodded.
'But Mrs Maguffy went after him?'
'Yes.'
The young man let his breath out, then said with a total conviction: 'So you've nothing whatever to worry about. That one knows her business and something to spare. Ten minutes to fix it at most and maybe less.'

Mary Maguffy had a split second to act but for a woman of

her special skills a split second was just enough. There was a table by the open door, a vase of chrysanthemums reflected in the mahogany. It was reflected and then it wasn't. She hadn't picked it up and thrown it, there hadn't been time for anything as deliberate, but her arm had come round in a slinging sweep and the palm of her hand had been open. The vase sprang off the table and Mary Maguffy after it. She had had no real hope of hitting the gun nor any real need to do so. A diversion was what she wanted and she made it. Kin had been aiming carefully and a flurry of flowers and porcelain had interrupted his line of sight. His trigger-finger checked instinctively and Mary Maguffy was on the gun. From the side—that was perfect. There was no sort of scuffle but a contemptuous expertise. One second Kin held the pistol, the next he didn't. The crash of the vase as it hit the mantel, the muffled thud of the gun as it dropped on the carpet, were simultaneous. Kin cried out in pain but swung at Mary. Which was exactly what she had hoped he would do. Off balance he hadn't a chance and she threw him painfully. She observed that he didn't know how to fall. She had plenty of time to pick up the gun. She picked it up and pocketed it.

She stood motionless, thinking. The immediate and material factors were all on her side. She had a gun now and Kin hadn't, and even without one she could have dealt with him very comfortably. So she could haul up Oliver Raden and lead him away: Kin couldn't interfere, he might not try. No, but he'd *know*. Here was a woman, dressed as an Auxiliary, and she'd disarmed him and thrown him heavily with an ease uncommon in the very best of Fire Services. And why wasn't she asking questions? Why was Raden going with her happily? Kin was a wholly detestable man who'd used torture and maybe intended worse but he hadn't the reputation of unintelligence; he'd put two and two together and arrive at the Executive. Mary was in a dilemma—she hadn't been briefed. She would have given her next weekend with Sergeant Maguffy for thirty seconds of Russell's counsel.

She stood in acute uncertainty but events resolved it for her.

Kin was already standing again and Oliver was shakily pulling himself to his feet. His face was the colour of week-old putty, he was fighting for breath, groaning between the uneven gasps, holding the back of a chair. From some well of courage he hadn't yet tapped he steadied himself and lifted the chair. He threw it at Kin, following in behind the flying chair in a blind bullock's clumsy rush.

Mary Maguffy watched with some detachment. They were fighting still with a shocking passion but she wasn't taking them too seriously. At the first sign of any real damage she could stop them and would do so. Meanwhile they were giving her time to think. Kin, shaken too, was giving ground slowly, blocking most of Oliver's blows but not quite all. He was the stronger man but much the smaller and Oliver Raden's round-arm swings were catching him on the ears and temples. Mary knew they would be painful, but you could hit for half an hour like that and a man would still be standing. One respectable punch. . . . She almost wished to see one, for this savage but ineffectual brawl offended her. But she had to decide what to do and it wouldn't come.

It never did but it didn't matter. Kin was backing still but slowly, seeking a lucky knee again, and as he moved a foot back he trod on the base of the broken vase. It was enough to destroy his balance and he dropped his hands instinctively. His head jerked back, his jaw jerked up, and a bucolic Raden hay-maker for once caught him squarely. Kin staggered across the room and finally fell. He fell with his head in the grate and he did not move.

Mary knelt down beside him but she knew before she touched his flesh. There'd been a sound she'd heard before and still remembered, the sickening crunch of skullbone smashed. She moved Kin's head an inch to make sure, then released it, not looking a second time. There was a cut steel fender, a beautiful thing, and the craftsman who'd made it had spared no love. Round its rim were small vases, Grecian she thought, and the vases had elegant pointed lids. One had impaled Kin's skull and one was plenty.

She got to her feet. 'He's dead,' she said.

Raden had picked up a piece of the vase. 'Ming,' he was saying softly, 'or something pretty close to it. Irreplaceable. A pity.'

'Kin's dead,' she said again, more sharply.

Oliver seemed half-dazed still. 'Yes? And so?'

'So it's somebody's lucky day and that's you and me.' She had realized at once that her decision had been made for her. Whatever strange angels watched ironically over the Executive had rung her up three cherries in line. 'Go to the car I told you about. Sheila's gone on already.'

He looked down at Kin. 'And him?'

'He was a horrible man who's had a horrible accident. He was trying to burn his papers in a panic and he slipped.'

'You can live with that?' Oliver was recovering with the quick resilience of the healthy male.

'I think we can.'

'The gun?' he asked unexpectedly.

'What gun?'

For the first time he smiled. 'If you say so. . . . Then I'm to go to that car still?'

'Get out of here before anyone sees us. Sheila has got news for you.'

'Are you all right yourself?'

'Of course I am.'

'Then thank you,' he said, 'for everything. Thank you for the Stag and thank you for getting us out of that cellar. Thank you finally for here and now.'

'Nothing. Goodbye. Good luck.'

He went past her without speaking again and she walked to the open safe. She'd noticed it and she knew what to do. Not the codes—that would be amateur. Secretly breaking a code was one thing, but if you knew that your codes had been stolen you simply changed them. But there'd be something in that safe worth an intelligent agent's attention. Mary looked inside it. There was a great deal of money in more than one currency and she knew better than to touch it. There were also two files with covers in Chinese characters and Mary couldn't read Chinese, but inside them there were photographs and Mary Maguffy could recognize several. She put the files in her shoulder bag. Charles Russell would be pleased with those files.

She looked round the room, checking as she'd been trained to. . . . A stiff's head in the grate but that could be acceptable as an accident. There were all the signs of panic, an open safe, some papers half burnt, a drawer of the desk left open, a broken vase. There was a chair overturned and that might be thought excessive. Mary replaced it carefully. . . . The gun? She had the gun. Oliver had been wearing gloves and so had she.

She gave the room a final searching stare. It wasn't a distinguished room but something distinguished had just occurred there. The wings of a simple justice had beaten powerfully in this little room, more than strongly enough to achieve what no Justice could have.

She suppressed the moral judgement since she'd been taught to eschew it on duty. As she went down the stairs in the thinning smoke a man in a bowler hat was coming up them. She'd been talking to him three hours ago but there wasn't a flicker of recognition.

She took a taxi to the Executive.

CHAPTER FIFTEEN

Charles Russell stayed on in his office that evening till well past seven. This was wholly exceptional. Across the street in Whitehall lights were still burning defiantly, senior civil servants awaiting the pleasure of overworked Ministers, not quite so senior civil servants who had finished their work and were reading the *Economist* but didn't like to go home lest they give the impression that they weren't entirely dedicated. But Russell went home at five thirty exactly, and if he stayed beyond that it meant something important. As indeed there was this evening. He was awaiting a visit from Chief Superintendent Willis and he was in excellent humour to cope with it.

One reason was a typewritten and unsigned note which had been delivered to him at six o'clock. *The most professional bit of arson I've ever seen. There will inevitably be suspicion but there was nothing found whatever to support it. My compliments to your boffin.* Reassured, though he'd never much doubted, Russell had then dealt with the political side as the experienced old hand he was. Harry Tuke had been on the telephone, his manner a mixture of undisguised relief and a vague uncertainty. And men with mixed emotions were easy game. Russell had played the relief and played it skilfully. . . . Yes, the news from Shahbaddin was very good. He quite saw that. Dictators might be unfashionable, but Sayed would be clever enough to avoid their more embarrassing excesses, and dictator or not he'd keep Shahbaddin where the Cabinet wanted it, still inside the Commonwealth. God alone knew why they wished such a thing but that wasn't Russell's business. And there'd been a fire at the High Commission? Yes, Russell had seen the evening paper. Also the High Commissioner had behaved most correctly, telephoning to the C.R.O. to compliment the Fire Service on its admirable promptitude and efficiency? How kind of him. Not that his view much mattered now, since certainly there'd be large changes in the staff of the High Commission. Sayed would see to that when he found the time. It was a pity that one of them had apparently panicked and broken his head in a careless fall, but Chinese were prone to panic as they were to other things less forgivable. So everything had turned out for the best.

. . . It had but it might go wrong again? How? There were two of the Radens in England still and Harry Tuke had been hearing rumours about some hoard of Raden gold which could be embarrassing? No doubt—Charles Russell saw that quite clearly. But it was a rumour at most and personally he didn't credit it. More important, the Radens weren't in England now.

They were.

They were not. They had left that evening privately.

There'd been a silence on the telephone, then an invitation to luncheon next day. Russell had accepted, but had reminded Tuke it was now his turn. At his own club then, and at one o'clock. That was convenient? Good.

Charles Russell had hung up and smiled. He found it perfectly convenient. Harry Tuke would be curious but Harry Tuke was a minister. Harry Tuke was on the pig's back now and he wouldn't risk a fall by tactless questions. The Minister was a veteran, a man you could do business with. Provided he needn't eat his food Russell enjoyed his company.

He smiled but collected his wits again. His interview with Willis would be less easy, for he couldn't escape the brutal fact that in the end he'd ignored his interests. He'd snatched Sheila and Oliver Raden from a police force which had wanted them, so he had still to make his peace with a valued friend.

When Willis arrived Russell poured a large and expiatory whisky. The Chief Superintendent never fenced with Charles Russell, knowing he wasn't in Russell's league; instead he offered an immediate opening. 'I hear there was a fire this evening in the Shahbaddin High Commission. In the course of it a man died.'

'Yes, I've heard the news. Apparently he panicked and started burning his secret papers. While doing it he seems to have slipped and knocked his brains out on a fender.'

'It was rather a pretty fender. Cut steel with those pointed knobs on—Adam urns, I think you call them. A very desirable piece of furniture but not a thing to fall on heavily. But the man's name was Kin and that's very convenient.'

'You mean to me?'

George Willis said stolidly: 'What the Executive finds convenient is nothing of my business. I meant convenient to the police.'

Russell refreshed the whiskies. 'You're going to tell me?'

'Certainly.' The Chief Superintendent thought, then began to explain deliberately. 'I told you that Geoffrey Addis had been digging on the Raden estate, where somebody interrupted him and beat him up severely. Naturally the local police have had a man by his bedside in waiting, and though he isn't yet sensible he'd been babbling in delirium. Very queer story indeed. I wouldn't relish it at all if Kin were alive still. Addis went down there to dig for that hypothetical gold, and he went at the instance of Mr Kin who had offered him money to find it. And certain, well, *satisfactions*, which I dare say you can guess at knowing the background. It isn't a pretty story.'

'No, it is not.'

'Our guess is that Kin double-crossed him on the job, so you could say that he got what he asked for. Which is more than his poor old father did. By the way, we fed the Coroner's jury on hints about domestic trouble, business falling away and so on. The rest didn't seem terribly relevant so the jury didn't hear it. They often don't in Coroners' courts. They brought in the soft verdict which was Balance of his Mind Disturbed.'

'I'm glad of that, he was a fine old man.'

'Who gat himself a bad one.'

'It goes like that sometimes, with cattle too. What'll happen to Mastertons?'

'Young Addis will have to sell it. That would have broken his father's heart but it won't break his. When he's paid the old man's debts there'll be something left.'

'Better than he deserves perhaps.'

'I'm a policeman, not a moralist. But returning to that beating-up, young Addis has been babbling about a Chinese in a stocking mask.' George Willis shrugged. 'I ask you. No fingerprints either. There are thousands of Chinese about—we haven't a hope of getting him. But Addis also mentioned Kin by name so you can see why his death is convenient. I've said this before but I'll say it again: next to bribery and a scandal there's just one thing a good policeman hates. That's poking about in embassies, questioning diplomatists. It's bad enough simply questioning them, but when one of them's suspect of ordinary crime it's an ordinary policeman's nightmare.'

'I can see that Kin's death is helpful.'

'It's been our lucky day there but there's something pretty embarrassing still. I mean the Radens—both of them. The civil case about that safe has been dropped, but it's humanly speaking certain the Radens blew it, and that's common crime in any known language. I told you I'd have to pull them in, but at twelve o'clock an Inspector goes down to Miss Raden's flat and they're neither of them there.' George Willis looked at Russell with an expression which straddled respect and resentment. 'You snatched them under my nose,' he said.

'Not quite like that. I considered it once since I believed they were both in danger, but you'd told me you meant to pull Sheila in and I try not to cheat my friends unless I have to. So I didn't snatch them but somebody else did.'

'Who?'

'Your Mr Kin. Or more accurately he snatched Sheila, and Oliver, a foolish man but a very brave one, followed her into the trap.'

'What was Kin going to do with them?'

'Get them out of the country quietly by threatening each that he'd torture the other. Then play it by the book and kill them. Formally that's guessing but I'm a pretty good guesser.'

There was a very long silence before George Willis spoke again. His face was quite expressionless but his shrewd eyes betrayed him; he would have liked to laugh but it wouldn't have been proper; he said finally, impersonally:

'So there was a fire in the High Commission.'

'There was a fire in the High Commission, yes.'

'In which Mr Kin had an unfortunate accident.'

'So you and the papers tell me.'

There was another friendly silence which Willis broke by asking, not quite so friendly: 'Where are the Radens now?'

'In Shahbaddin.'

'I could try for extradition, you know.'

'But I hope you won't.' Russell went over to a formidable safe, saying across his shoulder: 'I had to act in the end, though I can forgive you what you're thinking. But you know what's just happened in Shahbaddin and the Radens were much too hot to risk complications. Politics, the awkward bits—that's what I'm paid to stifle. So I snatched them when I had to but I'll try to pay my account with you.' He returned to the desk with two files which he handed Willis.

'I don't know Chinese.'

'You don't have to. We've done a quick translation of the bits that really matter. Read.'

Willis read for five minutes. At the end he said: 'God Almighty.'

'It isn't pretty, is it? That's how Kin's people got their funds. Drugs. Everything from pot to the really hard ones. It's all in those files—how they imported, the pushers, everything. You can mop up the lot.'

'And will,' Willis said. He thought, then added warily: 'You were talking about paying an account with me. And I was talking about the Radens whom you saw fit to whisk away from us.'

'That puts it a little crudely.'

'I'm a crude sort of man but I know a bargain when I see one. These files blow a drug ring wide open.' George Willis scratched an ear and grinned. 'Was I really going on about those Radens?'

'You were a bit.'

'Well, I don't think I'm too much interested in them now.'

When Willis had gone Russell began to write a letter. It was to Mary Maguffy and its manner was pleasantly formal. He'd be honoured by her company next evening. There was *Aida* at Covent Garden and Mrs Maguffy would enjoy it. The curtain went up at half-past seven, which was a barbarity which all deplored, so he suggested she have a sandwich first and he'd offer a proper meal afterwards.

He addressed the envelope carefully and sent for a safehand messenger. He then poured another whisky and drank it slowly. It was the fourth of the evening but for once he wasn't counting. It would serve till he got himself home to a civilized drink.

EPILOGUE

Outside the palace it was very quiet. It wasn't in fact a palace either architecturally or in its ambience but a comfortable hot-weather bungalow by the sea. The veranda was wide, the living-room really, and this evening a brisk breeze cooled it.

Sheila hadn't expected to see it again, thinking it had been sequestrated. Perhaps it had been once, she'd never know, for within hours of her arrival a smiling young Malay had conducted her to it formally. It was almost as she remembered it, even to some of the older servants. The young Malay had called her Princess, a form of address which much embarrassed her, and he'd embarrassed her further by hints about money. It had been done with some delicacy but the import had been clear. The country, he'd said, was enchanted to have a Raden back, but nowadays life was expensive. . . .

Sheila had said that she wasn't yet on the breadline. She had enough to live on in Shahbaddin, enough even to pay her taxes which most men didn't. And that didn't include the gold which had never been.

'What gold?'

'The gold you sent my cousin to find.'

'Oh that.' For a moment the young man's suavity dented; he said with unusual seriousness: 'There were rumours about that gold and we were forced to run them down. The money might have been useful too, but in the event we didn't need it. Now we're perfectly sure there was no such thing. It cost you and your cousin some trouble to find that out, but you can see how we were fixed when the rumours started. We had to be sure. Bazaar rumours. . . .' He shrugged. 'You'll know what they are, the damage they can do to any party.'

'I know. Bazaar rumours——'

'We leave it?'

'We leave it.'

Now she was in a long cane chair, waiting for Oliver Raden. He came in erect, his step light and springy, pulling another chair beside her own. His fear had gone and his tension with it.

'Imagine,' he said.

'Imagine what?'

'They've made me an acting minister. Services rendered, you know—I can't think what.' There was all his old sharp irony but no longer against himself. 'When there's an election I'll stand and become a proper one.'

'The Honourable Oliver Kendry?'

'No, just Oliver Raden.'

'I'm glad of that—it was a very poor joke. Everyone knew and nobody cared.'

'They're funny people,' he said reflectively. 'They killed your father who wouldn't go, and any Raden who tried to rule again couldn't hope to last a fortnight. But they're delighted to have us back on their own sweet terms. We're part of the scenery, part of their past, and they don't tear their roots up easily. A hundred-odd years of Radens. . . . In an odd sort of way they're really rather proud of us.'

'Hence Oliver Raden, budding minister.'

'Budding but with a string to it.'

'What's that?'

'They'd like to see me married,' he said. 'The line—all that.'

'Will you find that terribly difficult?'

'Would you?'

'What do you think?'

'I dare to hope.'

'I told you before, you're a terrible fool. All that nonsense about proving yourself——'

He looked at her once and once was enough. But he said: 'Not so fast, they made conditions.'

She said something very unladylike about men who made conditions.

'It wouldn't be a marriage of convenience, you know. There'd have to be a family, baskets and baskets of little Radens.'

'I wouldn't find that intolerable.' She rose lithely from the long cane chair and he rose too.

He carried her into the bungalow.